WAYFARER

WAYFARER
Book One of The Shekinah Chronicles

A Novel by
MATTHEW DICKENS

Cover Design By: Valor Comics, **MARIO RUIZ**
ValorComics.com

Destiny Image Fiction
An Imprint of
Destiny Image_fi Publishers, Inc.
P.O. Box 310
Shippensburg, PA 17257-0310

ISBN 0-7684-2238-8

For Worldwide Distribution
Printed in the U.S.A.

This book and all other Destiny Image, Revival Press,
MercyPlace, Fresh Bread, Destiny Image Fiction,
and Treasure House books are available at Christian
bookstores and distributors worldwide.

For a U.S. bookstore nearest you, call
1-800-722-6774.

For more information on foreign distributors, call
717-532-3040.

Or reach us on the Internet:
www.destinyimage.com

ENDORSEMENT

It is my joy to commend the writings of Matthew Dickens to you. In particular, I want to say a positive word about his newest work, Wayfarer. Anyone who reads this Christian fiction will be challenged to more carefully consider the glory of God and the evil world of Satan and the demonic that opposes His plan at every turn.

Matthew Dickens is a creative and gifted writer. His imagination, tempered by biblical truth, carries us into a spiritual dimension that challenges us to seriously consider the claims of Christ upon our lives. Matthew s writings are lively and engaging from beginning to end. No reader will be disappointed with what they find in these pages.

Dr. Daniel L. Akin
President, Southeastern Baptist
Theological Seminary
Wake Forest, NC

Character Descriptions

THE ORACLE

Applicable Biblical References:

Antichrist References:{Genesis 3: vs. 15; Psalm 10; Psalm 52: vs. 1-7; Psalm 55: vs. 11-14; Psalm 74: vs. 8-10; Psalm 140: vs. 1, 10, 11; Isaiah 10: vs. 5, 12; (Isaiah 14: vs. 1-11 and vs. 16-21: refer to the Antichrist.) Isaiah 16: vs. 4, 5; Isaiah 25: vs. 5; Isaiah 27: vs. 1; Isaiah 30: vs. 33; Jeremiah 4: vs. 7; Lamentations 4: vs. 11-12; Ezekiel 21: vs. 25-27; Ezekiel 28: vs. 1-8; Daniel 11: vs. 36; Amos 3: vs. 11; Micah 5: vs. 5-6; Nahum 1: vs. 11, 12, 15; Habakkuk 2: vs. 4-5; Zechariah 11: vs. 12-17; (Cross reference Zechariah 13: vs. 2 & Matthew 12: vs. 43-45:) John 17: vs. 12; Acts 1: vs. 25; II Thessalonians 2: vs. 3; Revelation 6: vs. 8; Revelation 9: vs. 11; Revelation 11: vs. 7; Revelation 14: vs. 18; Revelation 17: vs. 8; Revelation 19: vs. 20.}

Nephilim References: (Giants of the Naphal; also known as the gegenes gibborim.)(Genesis 6: vs. 1-4; Deuteronomy 3: vs. 1-11; I Samuel 17: vs. 1-51; I Chronicles 20: vs. 4-8; Jude: vs. 6-8.)

Lycanthropy References: (Shapeshifting.) (I Chronicles 11: vs. 22; Daniel 4: vs. 28-34; II Corinthians 11: vs. 14.)

THE SCROLL OF NAMES

The Trinity: (The Father, Son and Holy Spirit, also known as Us; see Genesis 1: vs. 26.)

The Father: (The Ancient of Days, the Father of Lights, Abba, the Spirit of

9

Adoption, Jehovah-Jireh, Lord and I am who I am.)

The Son: (Jesus, Immanuel, the Word, the Good Shepherd, Goel, Melchizedek, the Son of God, the Ancient of Days, the Son of Man, the Lion of the Tribe of Judah, the Christos Champion, The Living One, King of Kings and Lord of Lords, The Coming One and I am who I am.)

The Holy Spirit: (The Spirit of the Lord, the Spirit of Wisdom, the Spirit of Understanding, the Spirit of Counsel, the Spirit of Might, the Spirit of Knowledge and the Spirit of the fear of the Lord; see Isaiah 11: vs. 2)

Lucifer: (The Anointed Cherub, a Zoon or Ha-Seraph.)

Michael: (Archangel; the Great Prince who protects Israel.)

The Assassin: (A shadowy protector of Lucifer s Imperial Court.)

Gabriel: (A prince in the Order of the Watchers.)

Scriptos: (Keeper of the Shekinah Chronicles.)

Magnus the Lehohn: (The Shekinah Champion.)

Iscarius Alchemy: (The Son of Perdition.)

Simon Menelaus: (Master of the Harness Magi.)

Sodom: (A Shadow King in the Council of Thrones and Master of the Nekros Order.)

Tsavo: (A Nephilimite giant; the last progeny of the second preternatural race of supermen spawned by fallen angels after the Second Great Deluge.)

EMPIRES & HIERARCHIES

The Saints: (The Elect Ecclesia who will rule the universe in three distinct groups as regents of the Christos King; the earthly Jewish Wife {bethulah} the heavenly Jewish Bride {gune} and the Church. The Church is also known as the mystical Body of Christ, of which Christ is the Head.)

Archangel: (Crown Prince over all the elect angels in service to the Kingdom of God.)

Cherubim: (The living creatures who direct worship in Heaven and guard God s throne, also known as Seraphim or Zoa. Zoon, Seraph and Cherub are their singular designations. Seraph is also interchangeable with the word serpent in certain passages of Holy Writ, meaning shining or burning one. Compare Genesis 3: vs. 14-15, Numbers 21: vs. 6-9 and Isaiah 6: vs. 1-7.)

The Twenty-Four Elders: (Angelic rulers serving in the Kingdom of God.)

The Watchers: (The seven angels {*i.e. spirit beings or eyes*} standing before the throne of God in the Revelation of Jesus Christ; see Daniel 4 and Zechariah chapters 1-4.)

Book Masters: (Angels who record all that transpires in the whole of creation.)

Hosts: (Warriors also known as angels or the sons of God. They serve as guardians of the heirs of salvation.)

Council of Thrones: (Ten Shadow Kings ruling over the Kingdom of Darkness. The word king here is interchangeable with prince. It comes from the Hebrew word sar, which means ruler; see Daniel 10: vs. 13-21.)

Thrones: (Angelic rulers of the global order.)

Dominus: (Dominium Gate Masters guarding the entrances of galaxies and dominion pathways.)

Powers of the Air: (Rebel angels residing in the aerial regions.)

Demons: (Wicked spirits seeking union with mortals; also known as the Shedhim and the Seirim. They are not to be confused with rebel angels.)

The Locust Cherubim: (Winged, supernatural creatures with armored bodies shaped like horses that have the faces of men and hair like women flowing from beneath golden crowns, with each having tails like a scorpion; their likenesses possibly being linked to the post Flood Teraphim of the Assyrians. They are currently imprisoned in the Bottomless Pit.)

The Brimstone Cavalry: (A two hundred million strong army of fallen angels arrayed with breastplates of fire, jacinth and brimstone, riding upon horses that have lion-like heads and serpent-headed tails.)

The Euphrates Strongmen: (Four rebel angels bound in the Euphrates River, each waiting for the hour, day, month and year when they will be released to lead the Brimstone Cavalry in destroying a third of mankind; see Revelation 9: vs. 13-15.)

The Gegenes Kings: (Rulers from the third wave of Nephilimite giants to come.)

The Harness Magi: (An ancient guild of warrior priests and assassins. They also serve as guardians of the Covenant Harness.)

The Illuminati: (An elite class of men who control the worlds Central Banks, also known as the International Bankers or Rex Deus; a coven of sorcerers falsely claiming descent from the House of King David, with key bases of operation located in Rhodes, Malta, London, Jupiter Island and New Haven, Connecticut.)

The Masonic Order: (A Luciferian cult of cabalistic mysticism controlled by the Illuminati.)

The Vampire Demoniacs: (Covens of demon possessed men and women.)

The Idumaean Council of Princes: (The royal houses of Europe with blood-line links to the Herodian Dynasty and members of the Illuminati)

Apostate Israel: (Those of the Israelite nation who reject the Messiah.)

The Great Tree: (The cedar of world government embodied in the Assyrian and his elect kings.)

Assyria: (The restructured Levant land bridge, and one of the empires beneath the boughs of the Great Tree, with capitals in Babylon, Tyre and Pergamos.)

The Omega Group: (A multibillion dollar megacompany created by the Harness Magi that has its international headquarters in the Turkish city of Pergamos.)

Alpha Corps: (A covert army of Red Horse Units created by the Omega Group.)

Shadow Corps Intelligence: (An intel agency created by the Omega Group.)

Wolf Pack: (Twelve man Special Op units assembled by the Omega Group; the tip of the spear.)

Sentinel Corps: (Security forces providing protection for the Omega Group s corporate offices and international projects.)

Special Services: (An elite communications and electronic countermeasures team created by the Omega Group.)

NGOs: (Non governmental organizations allied to the Omega Group and the Illuminati.)

COSMIC EMPIRES

The Kingdom of God: (The universal kingdom.)

The Kingdom of Heaven: (Also known as the Millennial Kingdom; a period of time when the Lord Jesus will unite with Israel and reign over the Earth for one thousand years. This is the subject of the Lord Jesus marturia testimony in the four Gospels and the Revelation.)

Heaven: (The glorious land.)

Outer Realm: (The circular universe beyond Earth controlled mainly by Lucifer and his fallen hosts who make up the Kingdom of Darkness, with rebel strongholds set up on barren planets and asteroids throughout space to block the Parade Route of the prophesied Conqueror to come.)

Earth: (The jewel of contention in the circular universe.)

New Jerusalem: (A jeweled city of cubicle design reaching fourteen hundred miles high, long and wide, nestled within a hovering sphere of transparent gold with a circumference measuring over eight thousand miles; the future capital of the universe. Its current location is in an undisclosed region within Heaven until the day of its earthly inauguration after the millennial reign of the Lord Jesus and his final judgment on the wicked.)

EMPIRE HOLDINGS

Abraham s Bosom: (A place of rest located in the same region as Hades, but is separated from the torments section by a great gulf; see Luke 16 vs. 19-31.)

Dragylon: (The Imperial Fortress of the Archrebel, which has its docking port in the airspace over Pergamos.)

Hades: (Also known as Sheol or *The Grave*; a temporary prison of torments for the damned located in the bowels of the Earth, controlled by the Kingdom of God.)

The Abyss: (A place of confinement for demons and rebel angels that fall in battle; see Luke 8 vs. 26-33.)

The Well of the Abyss: (Also known as the Bottomless Pit; a place of confinement for the Unclean Spirit, the Locust Cherubim and the Brimstone Cavalry.)

Hell: (Also known as the Lake of Fire; the final destination of the damned judged on the day of the second resurrection at the Great White Throne Judgment.)

WORLDS

The Pre-Adamic World: (The original Earth where Lucifer was the Anointed Cherub of the threefold district of God s first Edenic Empire, the districts being Eden, the Garden of God and the Holy Mountain, foreshadowing the Outer Court, the Holy Place and the Holy of Holies in the Jewish Tabernacle and the Temples of Solomon and Zerubbabel. Applicable references can be found in Genesis 1: vs. 1-2; Isaiah 14: vs. 12-15; Ezekiel 28: vs. 11-19. Genesis 1: vs. 2 reads in the Hebrew, *The Earth became waste and a ruin*, which was caused by Lucifer s rebellion as shown in the other passages.)

The Adamic World: (The refurbished Earth where Adam and Eve walked in the Garden of God until sin entered in and caused the Fall of Mankind.)

The Antediluvian World: (The Middle East region and adjacent Nephilimite territories in the Levant Land Bridge destroyed during the flood of the Second Great Deluge.)

The Ancient World: (Land regions of the post Flood era where the focus of history was primarily on Africa, the Middle East and Asia Minor.)

The Old World: (The continent of Europe.)

The New World: (The continents of North, Central and South America.)

THE ARMORY

The Sword of the Lord: (A seismic power of earthly and supernatural destruction.)

Dragaduceus: (The war-blade of the Dragon Lord.)

The Covenant Harness: (A covenant garment of global power.)

The Oracle of the Dragon Lord: (An ancient staff of cosmic power wielded by the Masters of the Harness Magi.)

The Trumpet of the Lord: (A theocratic trumpet of cosmic ascension and assembly wielded by Prince Gabriel from the Order of the Watchers.)

Preternatural Weapons: (All manner of weapons forged with natural and preternatural materials such as swords, sickles, shields, armor, trumpets, crossbows, stellar explosives, flying chariots and galactic siege machines.)

Adamantine: (A preternatural metal of varying colors with great density and flexibility; an alloy that also served as the mold for the earthly Damascus Steel.)

Christaloy: (An alloy of different colors that is harder than adamantine.)

POWERS OF THE SHEKINAH CHAMPION
Applicable Biblical References:

Immortal lifespan: (Genesis 3: vs. 22, Genesis 5: vs. 27.)

Indestructible against mortal weapons: (Isaiah 54: vs. 17.)

Seeing the supernatural: (Genesis 28: vs. 12; II Kings 6: vs. 16-17; Revelation: chapters 1-22.)

Wrestling with the supernatural: (Genesis 32: vs. 24-30.)

Supernatural speed: (I Kings 18: vs. 44-46; Psalm 18: vs. 33.)

Supernatural hearing: (I Thessalonians 4: vs. 15-18.)

Seismic power harnessed in voice: (Psalm 18: vs. 7, 8; Matthew 27: vs. 50-51; John 18: vs. 6.)

Supernatural strength and cunning: (Judges 14: vs. 5-6; Judges 15: vs. 14-16; Judges 16: vs. 28-30; I Chronicles 11: vs. 10-24.)

The ability to fly: (II Kings 2: vs. 11; Psalm 18: vs. 29; Acts 1: vs. 9-11; Acts 8: vs. 39.)

The ability to use his powers at will: (Revelation 11: vs. 6.)

Wrath in the Church Age: (Romans 13: vs. 4; I Thessalonians 4: vs. 6.)

THE SHEKINAH LEGACY

Lucifer: (The first created champion of the Shekinah Legacy who brought desolation and darkness to the universe when trying to obtain equality with God.)

18

Moses: (A son of the House of Levi; the first to inherit the restructured mantle of the Shekinah Legacy who led the nation of Israel from Assyro-Egyptian bondage.)

Joshua: (The son of Nun whose father was a prince in the House of Ephraim; a champion who led the Jewish invasion of the Promised Land.)

Othniel: (The son of Kenaz; a champion and Judge of Israel who brought peace to Israel for 40 years after defeating King Cushan-Rishathaim of Mesopotamia.)

Ehud: (The left-handed son of Gera the Benjamite; a champion who brought peace to Israel for 80 years after slaying Eglon the fat King of Moab and leading the destruction of 10,000 of Moab s stout men of valor.)

Shamgar: (The son of Anath; a champion who slew 600 men with an ox goad.)

Barak: (The son of Abinoam of Kedesh; a champion who, with the guidance of Deborah the Judge, led the nation of Israel in a great victory over Sisera of Harosheth Hagoyim and his lord King Jabin of Canaan that brought peace to the land for 40 years.)

Gideon: (The son of Joash the Abiezrite; a champion who led 300 men in a great victory against the Midianites and the Amalekites that brought peace to Israel for 40 years.)

Tola: (The son of Puah of Issachar; a champion who judged Israel for 23 years.)

Jair: (A son of Gilead who judged Israel for 22 years.)

Jephthah: (A son of Gilead who was born of a harlot; a champion who judged

19

Israel for 6 years and wrought a great victory against the Ammonites and the rebels of the House of Ephraim.)

Ibzan: (A champion from Bethlehem who judged Israel for seven years.)

Elon: (A champion from Zebulun who judged Israel for 10 years.)

Abdon: (The son of Hillel the Pirathonite; a champion who judged Israel for eight years.)

Samson: (A Nazarite from the womb who was the son of Manoah the Danite; a champion who judged Israel for 20 years and began to deliver them with great victories against the Philistines.)

Samuel: (The son of Elkanah of the House of Ephraim; a champion of judgment and prophecy who helped establish the monarchy of Israel by anointing Saul and David as kings over Israel during his life on Earth.)

King David: (The son of Jesse of the House of Judah; a champion of the greatest renown who reigned over Israel for 40 years, a throne to be established forever.)

The Davidic 37: (Thirty-seven champions fiercely loyal to King David who wrought great victories during the king s reign; some having slain hundreds of men at once while fighting alone.)

Magnus the Lehohn: (A prince in the House of Sheshbazzar and a member of the Shekinah Legacy who would foreshadow the return of the Christos Champion.)

*"If a trumpet is blown in a city,
will not the people be afraid?
If there is calamity in a city,
will not the Lord have done it?"*

Amos 3: vs. 6

PROLOGUE:

The mouth of hell was bright with moonlight, shining the way for a gilded transport making its way through the spirit-filled night along the eastern boundary road of the Hinnom Valley; an ancient hole in the ground of human torment just outside the gates of Jerusalem. The transport was pulled along the road at a generous speed by a team of Friesian horses, escorted on all sides by a *quingenary* unit of Roman Cavalry known as the *Ala Quingenaria*. Banners bearing the crest of the House of Octavius flew near each corner of the transport s rectangular roof, billowing softly in the night wind as they mixed with the rest of the ensign-crowned poles being carried by the *quingenary s* other standard bearers.

A woman and her young son sat inside the transport s purple-padded interior, partially illuminated by moonlight filtering through small openings in the heavy drapes framing the windows. The woman was beautiful with smooth, milky skin and long red hair braided with gold rings, which draped down through the hood of her blue, palla cloak layered in folds over her white stola. She sat silently reading a scroll sent to her in Rome by her husband before his assassination several months ago, an act which also took the life of her firstborn. He had implored her to bring their younger son to Jerusalem for the Passover Feast.

Her youngest sat beside her solemnly playing a Jewish kinnor; a ten-stringed, pentatonically- tuned instrument he strummed with plectrums made of smooth bone. He was dressed in a white mantle with rainbow colored strips of cloth sewn around the edges of its large sleeves, a coat of many colors his father had given to him a year ago. A necklace with a round emblem made of pure gold hung from his neck, the bronze lion engraved in its center representing the royal seal of the House of Sheshbazzar; a line of nobility descending from the House of David.

The dark-haired boy stopped playing suddenly as an unearthly chill sifted through the transport s purple curtains, bristling the hairs on the back of his neck with a familiar feeling of dread.

He stared blankly into the cold shadows on the left. Tears trickled slowly from his emerald eyes as he clutched the kinnor close to his chest like a shield. It was as if some hungry predator lurked unseen in the shadows of the transport s interior; a recurring fear that was always coldest in his bedchambers at night, stalking him with whispers of a sharpened hate.

His mother turned to him when she noticed his playing had stopped, surprised by the tears streaming down his face. She laid the scroll aside and cupped his face in both her hands, turning it toward her. What s the matter, my precious? she asked.

His eyes trembled slightly as he looked up into his mother s flawless face glowing in the moonlight. Abba.... I.... I miss Abba and James, he said.

She wiped away the tears on her son s cheeks with loving strokes of her soft thumbs. I miss them, too, my Lehohn.

The boy bowed his head with a sudden look of shame when his mother addressed him by the proud surname given to him at birth. I m sorry, mother, he said.

For what, my child?

For crying.

She lifted his chin gently, smiling with a look of supreme adoration. Tears are not shameful, my son, she told him, her eyes brightening with a tender passion. You have your father s heart. He was a compassionate man. A prince in the Tribe of Judah. That, as well as his and your brother s faith in this Christos Champion they were always writing to us about, is what made them such a threat to King Herod.

25

The boys eyes hardened through his tears suddenly at the mention of Herod Antipas, remembering his grandfather s words to his mother and him about how the Idumean King had hired an assassin to murder his father and brother.

I hope Herod lives a long life, he said sharply.

The woman looked at her son with surprise. What prompts you to wish that wicked king such fortune, my son?

That I may avenge Abba and James with my own hands, he replied.

Vengeance is never the way, my son, she warned. Blood is easily spilled. But it is not easily forgotten when it is done for personal gain. Be careful in what manner you choose to expose its color to your eyes.... Remember, you are the rightful heir to the throne of Judah now. How you govern your actions in personal affairs will determine whether or not you will rule as a wise king one day.

The boys eyes fell from his mothers face.

Look at me, my son.

His movement was slow, tears streaming down his cheeks.

She cupped her hands around his face again, wiping away his tears in the same manner as before. Your grandfather is a very powerful man in the Roman Senate, she reminded him. He has told me more than once that Tiberius days as emperor

are numbered. He is also allied to the ene-
mies of Antipas that roam the halls of
power in Rome, especially Herod s
nephew Agrippa. He will see to it justice is
done once Tiberius is gone, and Antipas no
longer has an ally on the throne. Mean-
while, you must focus on your future,
which will begin in part with your probatio
training that will teach you the ways of the
Roman Army. You will become an artisan
of war and politics to prepare you for a
future throne of your own. But you must
never forget who you are. That is why I
have brought you to Jerusalem for your
first Passover.

I will be a good king, mother, he
said eagerly. I will.

She smiled, pulling him close to her
chest to hug him tightly. I know you will,
my Lehohn, she said, kissing him softly
on top of the head. Just remember what
your father always taught you, *Out of the
mouth of babes and nursing infants God
has ordained strength....* Strength that
will silence the enemy and the avenger.

―――•◦◦•―――

A towering figure with wide shoulders and dark, collar-length hair stood in
the center of the transport s rectangular
roof, his burnished face emanating a
bronze glow. He was dressed in a robe of
royal-blue flax that shimmered in the
moonlight. A linked belt of golden eyes

27

was fastened around his tapered waist, supporting a broadsword in a silver sheath the size of a weaver's beam. A white pouch was nestled next to the sword on his belt, containing dozens of stellar explosives in the shape of small silver balls. On the right side of his belt was an ivory inkhorn and a large square holster containing a crimson-colored book of historical accounts about heroes and monsters, each bound by an ancient legacy.

Spirals of silver light filtered from the sides of his bright eyes as he stared up at the heavens. The clatter of shifting suits of armor filled the night air from the dust forces of the *Ala Quingenaria* traveling along in their formations on all sides of him, oblivious to his presence on the roof of the transport.

He slipped his hand over the hilt of his sword while watching a vast stream of rebel angels pass by above him, their eyes burning with red and yellow fires. He remained invisible even to them due to a special angelic and cherubic diffraction veil he was cloaked in, which allowed him to move unseen for long periods of time throughout the hidden realm.

A chorus of piercing howls filled the night air as packs of wolves in the surrounding hills announced the invisible approach of the powers of darkness, alerting the transport's armor-clad guardians to a more diligent watch of the shadowy groves of trees on each side of the road. Many of the rebel hosts landed on the spire-bordered roof of Zerubbabel s refurbished Temple rising into the night sky like a gold and marble beacon. Others took up positions on the battlements of the eastern wall looming high above the valley road, crowding together on the parapets between the blazing watch fires that cast ghostly spirals of light on the slope below, each anticipating a devilish spectacle to come.

The wingless angel glanced at the roof beneath his boots. His commission to protect and monitor the young prince below was about to carry him into the heart of darkness once more as it had done so often in the past. But on this night, the angels of the Archrebel would focus the brunt of their destructive ways on the Christos Champion who had turned Jerusalem upside down with his messianic proclamations of divinity and salvation.

Warnings to you, Book Master, a cold voice echoed suddenly from behind. As the heavens are high and the Abyss is deep, so you can be sure that I haven t forgotten about the young prince in your keep.

The angel snapped his head up in a look of surprise, abruptly turning to face a legendary assassin who was both feared and respected throughout the ranks of holy and rebellious angels alike. He was a mountain of carved muscle, hovering near the roof between two of the cavalry s pole standards rising up behind the rear corners of the transport, his towering form glistening with a black, marble-like sheen in the moonlight. Slanted eyes of white fire glowed in the shadow masking his face, framed with golden locks of translucent hair. Sharply-tipped wings of bronze-colored adamantine protruded from his back, curving around his expansive shoulders in a liquid motion. Frigid vapors rolled down the vertical spines bulging from the exterior and interior of his metallic wingspan, spiraling around silver icons similar to the last letter of the Greek alphabet that were engraved hundreds of times between the spines of each wing.

The angel took a step back on the roof, clutching the breast of his robe, wondering if the assassin could really see him as he stared at the shadow masking his face.

Worry not about your cloak, scribe. It remains in-tact, said the assassin, a vampiric smile of diamond teeth flashing into view beneath his white eyes. But you can be sure that I can sense your confused presence.

The assassin hovered forward a pace, his smile increasing to a jester s width, eyes riveted on the space between the two banners flying near the opposite corners

of the transport s roof. Dark deeds tran-
spire tonight, do they not, scribe?

The angel s only reply was to grip the
hilt of his broadsword.

The assassin s long hair swished back
and forth around the sides of his shadowed face while he spoke, eyes flashing
brighter with each word. The hour of our
casting out has come. But it is only temporary. For I assure you of this, the Heir will
not make it to the *xulon* tree, he vowed.
He will not be allowed to fulfill his mission. He will either die by stones, or the
scourging of leather-wrapped bones. I will
see to that myself. Just as I will see to it
that the young prince in your charge below
doesn t fulfill his preordained path.

The assassin hovered forward a few
more feet, drawing closer to the spot
where he sensed the angel. There is only
one true champion. He was the first. The
Anointed Cherub. The young one you protect will become a son of my heritage.
Then he will die like the others before him.
This I prophesy to you. For the shadow of
the Dragon Lord s mark is already upon
him, he declared, pointing to a bronze,
two-headed dragon posted on top of an
insignia pole being carried by a *vexillarius*
standard bearer.

There is betrayal in the night s air,
scribe. Can you feel it?... Can you feel the
approaching destruction that promises to
have its sway over the Shekinah Legacy?

He glanced up at the sky, laughing softly as the rebel hosts continued to streak towards Jerusalem. Yes, he said, lowering his gaze again. Even now the Son of Perdition proceeds with the deed of all deeds. A deed that will bring him into a dark and secret place to prepare him for the *Covenant Harness*.

The assassin threw open his wings suddenly, reflecting the moonlight in a bronze flare while floating backwards from the roof of the transport. Remember this, Book Master, he said sharply. The allure of silver is always brightest when offered in the darkness of opportunity. Opportunity prophesied and undenied. Prophecy fulfilled, yet doomed by unconquerable scheme and pride.

His laughter echoed through the air as a torrent of shadows spiraled up around him from the bottom tips of his marked wings. He vanished on the spot when the dark shapes exploded outward with smoky flakes of frigid light.

The flakes faded in front of the angel, giving rise to a prophetic tone in his voice just as the wolves in the surrounding hills unleashed their dreaded wails through the night air. It begins.

Book I

ORIGINS I:
LEGACY

A lone warrior stood on a crag of rock that jutted out from the slope of Mount Scopus; a northern extension of the Mount of Olives also known as Lookout Hill that rose above the ancient city of Jerusalem. He was a statue of silence as he lingered in front of a thin grove of trees, gazing by the light of the moon at the watch fires burning on the siege banks built up between the broken walls of Rome s most turbulent province below.

The warrior, known as Magnus the Lehohn, wore fame and fierceness like few before him. Respect and honor had pursued him like a suitor since his graduation from the *probatio* training camps of the legionnaires. He would become the strongest and most cunning Praefectus Equitum in the *Alae Milliariae*, Rome s elite cavalry unit. To the dismay of family and friends, though, he had turned down posts in the Imperial Service and a seat in the senate offered to him on several occasions by the Emperor Vespasian himself for his years of decorated service to the empire. He had chosen to remain an officer in the *cohorts* until he could finish out his term of service. His desire was to terminate his association with the evil oaths and icons associated with the Roman Army once and for all. Too often had his faith in the risen Christ clashed with such ideologies like the Mithraism cult of the Persian sun god introduced to the empire by the eastern legions that had helped bring Vespasian to power.

Though in his forties, Magnus looked and lived with the vigor of a hearty young man of thirty. The younger men in his *cohort* units would never forget the day when they saw him chasing a band of zealots on his horse at full gallop. He had come upon their flank as he chased them into a ravine, stooping dangerously low from his horse to grab a young, well-built zealot in full armor by the ankle, snatching him straight up into the air as he righted himself in the saddle with ambidextrous ease. It was a feat only one other in their ranks was known to have matched. Such horsemanship was first developed during the summers of his youth that were spent on his grandfather s stud farm famously known throughout the empire for its highly valued breed of centinarius champions.

Magnus stood six feet tall, a height that had helped him advance through the ranks when he was younger. His collar-length hair was black and wavy, arms hard and well-defined, tanned to a deep color of bronze from many years spent in the sun. Their strength had been forged during his post *probatio* days in the portable, thatch-covered arenas of the *hippika gymnasia*, a sporting competition waged between Rome s elite officers. A sleeveless, leather tunic mounted with bronze scales adorned his torso, with a purple-hooded cloak spilling gracefully over the armor s bulging shoulders. An auxiliary belt with silver squares was strapped around his waist, supporting a cavalry spatha; a slashing blade with an ivory, finger-grooved hilt. A Thracian scabbard of pure gold, pierced and engraved with scenes from some of the more famous battles he had fought in, sealed the weapon from view. Leather straps were wrapped tightly around his calves, extending down to his spiked, ankle-high boots.

Tears glistened in Magnus emerald eyes while staring at the besieged and starving city below. Hundreds of zealots were impaled on both sides of the torch-lined road leading to the northern gate. The city s outer and secondary walls had been breached after five months of pounding by Scorpion catapults and other siege machines. The formidable tenth legion held the territory at the eastern extension of the Mount of Olives. The strongest portions of the army, though, had been lined

up seven legions deep in a fortified position in the Kidron Valley below before
moving in through the breaches in the city
walls, with three ranks of his own cavalry
units pulling up the rear behind them.
Reserve camps stationed at the foot of
Mount Scopus had all but been emptied in
the conquest of the Antonia Fortress; the
most strategic stronghold of the Jews. But
the final assault was still to come, an
assault on the Temple itself. And sadly, his
wife, along with many others, were, for all
he knew, still trapped in their homes near
the Temple Mount between the forces of
the zealots and those of the advancing
legions. All that he held dear in the world
was literally crumbling before him under
the iron heel of the Roman Empire. An
empire he had served valiantly since his
first day in the *probatio* training camps.

Magnus leaned his head against the
lance in his right hand, praying that his
wife Rachel was still alive somewhere. He
hadn t seen her since Rome s war with
Israel s zealots began four years ago. Many
had been trapped in the city at the beginning of the siege which came while they
were celebrating the Feast of the Passover.
He had secretly sent a messenger to his
wife before the siege began, giving him a
wooden slat with a fragment from part of
Luke s Gospel cryptically urging her to flee
to the mountains without betraying the
military stratagems of his superiors. But

38

confirmation of her having received the message never came. Such uncertainty about her whereabouts made his prayers all the more desperate.

I believe you made a request to see me.

Magnus whipped around in surprise. There on the rocky slope before him stood the second most powerful man in the Roman world. He was a handsome, well-built man, arrayed in a crimson cloak and a gold breastplate of muscular design. A parazonium sword was strapped around his waist, a dress weapon of Romano-Hellenic design used only by generals and governors. The light of the torch he was holding illuminated his rugged face and his short hair.

General Titus, said Magnus, snapping his weapon back against his shoulder, lightly rapping the scales of his *lorica* armor with a fisted salute as he acknowledged the Imperial Son. I didn t notice your approach from below.

Titus made his way through the grove of olive trees to where Magnus stood in a small clearing. I came along the eastern slope after my inspection of the tenth legion, he said.

I thank you for coming, general.

Only you, Magnus the Lehohn, could even presume to summon the son of Vespasian, he remarked.

Magnus smiled slightly, glancing past the Imperial Son at the guard detail lingering a few yards up the slope, with an old man standing in front of them.

The old man walked down to Titus side when Magnus focused on him, stepping into the light of the general s torch. He was of formidable stature and build for his age, dressed in the sacerdotal robes of the Jewish priesthood, a white beard and a shaggy mane of hair covering his face and head.

I believe you know Josephus, Titus remarked, gesturing to the old man at his side.

We have never met, Magnus replied. But I have often heard the deeds of the warrior priest who chose surrender rather than slaughter.

Josephus nodded warily. I never surrendered my heart, said the old man. I surrendered to sense, and to the academia of preserving my people and their history.

The old priest smiled with admiration at the hardened warrior before him. But I think our people would have probably fared better under your leadership, brave prince, he continued, revealing his knowledge of the warrior s lineage in the House of Sheshbazzar. I have seen and heard the deeds of Magnus the Lehohn as well. Your fame and nobility are even greater than that of Julian of the tenth legion.

Your words are kind, priest, he said. But fame in war is not the subject I wish to discuss at this hour.

Magnus turned his attention to Titus with a look of urgency. I was hoping to speak with you privately, general.

Titus waved to his Praetorian Guard stationed beyond the grove. Escort the scribe back to the Antonia Fortress, he ordered. I will follow later.

Josephus nodded at the general and started back up the slope. He stopped short, however, and turned back around towards Magnus. I have one question for you, Magnus, he said. Who gave you the surname Lehohn?

My father, he answered. It means *lion* in Greek.... The symbol of my father s house.

I know.... And it suits you well since your first name means *great*.

The old priest looked at the hardened warrior with a wild an ominous assurance in his eyes. I once saw a vision in the heavens before this war started, he remarked. It was a group of stars in the shape of a sword. I thought it to be a sign from God that a champion would arise and deliver the people of Israel. And now I know that I was partially right. For he has raised up a champion. Only he has not come to bring deliverance.... But judgment.

Josephus turned and started back up the slope in a slow stride. I will not soon forget you, *Great Lion,* the old priest told him, glancing back over his shoulder as he stopped again. And neither will the world. Your name will be immortal in the pages of history.

Magnus said nothing, giving only a respectful nod to the old priest before he turned away again and joined the Praetorian Guard beyond the grove.

The detail turned in a clatter of clanging armor as the priestly scribe joined their numbers again, marching back to their horses stationed several yards away on a higher ridge. The torchline above their heads faded slowly from view as they mounted their steeds and rode away towards the main path down the mountain.

Titus took several more steps down the slope until he was only a couple of feet from Magnus, propping his hand on the pommel of his sword as he locked gazes with the warrior. I can see the concern in your eyes, Magnus, he noted, the light of his torch illuminating both of their faces. This campaign is a difficult one for you, is it not?

To be sure, general.

I understand, he said. However, you are the most highly decorated Praefecti in the Imperial Army.... Your father may have been a prince in the Tribe of Judah, but your mother was the daughter of a Roman Senator. Don t let the dynasty of a broken kingdom cloud your judgment. Its days of glory will never come again.

Magnus pulled a small leather pouch from his auxiliary belt. Several pieces of silver could be seen peeking through an opening at the top of the pouch. I will always belong to the House of Sheshbazzar, he replied, looking back up at Titus. But fear not, general. I am of Solomon s lineage, and merely a prince of the royal bloodline, as my father and brother before me. I have no claim to the throne because of the past sins of King Jehoiachin.... The last and greatest of all the kings of Israel came through David s other son Nathan. He was a *Root* from a powerless and *dry ground* that had become the line of David. This was something my mother did not understand when she was grooming me for the throne of Israel. But I know my place now, and I hold no allegiance to the zealots who wish to control my homeland.... All wickedness in Jerusalem must be wiped away.

And what, to you, is wicked in fair Jerusalem, Magnus?

The plague of apostasy, sire, he answered, clinching the pouch in his hand tighter. I remember when my mother brought me back to Jerusalem as a boy at my father s request to experience my first Passover. And though it was against Jewish tradition to tabernacle among Gentiles during the celebration, my mother felt it would be safer to stay at the Atonia Fortress, due to the hostility shown to my fathers house by King Herod. And it was there that I first saw the Son of the living God. The last and greatest King of Israel who came through Nathans line.

You mean the Carpenter from Nazareth?

Yes, he answered, turning sideways to gaze at the city below. I watched from a secluded place in the Praetorium as he was interrogated by Pilate and scourged mercilessly under that cruel art of the *flagrum taxillatum*.

Magnus opened the pouch in his hand, letting the Imperial Son see one of the shekels inside that was engraved with the right profile of the curly-haired image of the Phoenician god Melkart on the shekels obverse, with an eagle standing on the rudder of a ship inscribed on the reverse side. These thirty shekels of Tyrian silver, the price of a slave as Moses and the Prophet Zechariah once wrote about, is what the Sanhedrin paid to betray their own Messiah. My mother obtained them from a merchant who had sold his potters field to the Sanhedrin for the same shekels forsaken by the Masters betrayer. She d heard how the chief priests had refused to keep blood money. Considering my father and brother were followers of Jesus, she sought out the merchant who had sold his field and made him an offer for the shekels he couldn t refuse. She often used them during my childhood education as tutorial reminders of the price of cowardice and betrayal. They were lessons meant to prepare me for the dangers of leadership.

Magnus paused, remembering every detail of the day his Savior died for him.

With my mother s approval and the commission of a small detachment of the *Ala Quingenaria,* he continued, we followed Jesus from the Gabbatha Pavement after he was sentenced to death. The mob celebrating his death sentence followed as well. Never had I seen such hatred and cruelty from the kinsmen of a condemned man before. The spirit of *Death* was everywhere, rolling with a crushing pitch that was barely kept at bay by the soldiers assigned to the execution detail. But Jesus remained utterly determined during his march to Golgotha. I have seen much in my warlike days, but I have never seen anyone suffer like he did, and then die with such heroism and power. The whole Earth shook at his passing.

But it didn t end there, he added. I didn t see it with my own eyes, but I know he rose from the dead, just as the Apostle Paul told me years ago. For the Spirit of the Lord bears witness with mine that he is seated in glory. He will return to this world at the appointed time to fulfill his Word, and to bring forth the righteousness of his rule.

I have heard the story of this ... new god, Titus spat out. His followers have spread this doctrine to the four corners of the Roman world. But my father is the ruler of all men, as it was prophesied when he received divine visions in the Temple of Serapis. It would not bode well for the rest of your military career to forget that, especially considering Rome s distaste for this new Jewish religion.

This is not a religion, sire, Magnus replied. He is *The Way*. He is God incarnate. He forgave me of all my sins.... It is through him that I have eternal life.

As you say, he replied with a wave of his hand. Just remember where your loyalties are rooted.

I will, general. Magnus turned around fully towards the city. As I said before, I have no allegiance to the apostasy of Israel. And I hold no loyalties toward the zealots and their guild of Sicarii assassins that are trying to revive the glory of the past, he assured him. I only wish that my wife, and others who have no part in this conflict, be spared from death.

Titus stepped to Magnus side, resting his hand on the warrior s shoulder. I have done all I could to preserve the lives of the innocent already, he answered, his face hard and remorseless in the light of his torch. These zealots have been deceptively barbaric from the start, though.

They do not abide by the rules of war. And because of it, I have been forced to treat them in the same manner. But I will do what I can to make sure nothing foul befalls your precious Rachel. If she is still alive as you hope.

Magnus looked into Titus stern face, a small gleam of hope in his emerald eyes. He wasn t sure if he could trust the general to take such measures in the heat of war. And though Titus was greatly loved and respected by his men, he still remembered how brutally the general had treated his own soldiers whenever they were put to flight by the zealots during a battle.

Magnus held the general s quiet stare while he pondered those realities. He also knew of Titus rumored dislike for having to tolerate a half-Jew in the hierarchy of his army s command structure. The rumor had spread throughout the Imperial Army shortly after the beginning of the siege. But the general vigorously denied the rumor when approached about it. Instead, Titus lauded him with praise and assurance that he held the same respect for him as the rest of the empire did.

In the end, however, it didn t really matter what Titus thought of him. He was a freed man in the risen Christ. Because of this, he was compelled to do what was right, even in war. By that compulsion, he himself would protect as many of the innocent as possible.

General, said a voice from behind.

Magnus and Titus turned at the sound of a gruff voice coming from the upper side of the grove. The silhouette of a towering figure captured their gazes as it emerged into the light of Titus torch. He stood two feet taller than Magnus, chest wide and heaving, arms long and sinewy, his streamlined jaw covered by a thin black beard. His dark olive, skin glistened with a watery sheen. A long mane of braided black hair dangled to his waist. His silver breastplate was ancient Egyptian, with gold eagle wings crossing at the center. A white schenti skirt with sheer-like pleats was fitted around his waist, splitting up the middle to reveal a blue tunic of the same material. A curved shotel sword hung from his jewel-studded belt.

Magnus stood amazed at the warriors unusual size. Never had he seen the likes of such a man before as they locked gazes.

You must not travel alone in these parts, general, the giant urged, his voice deep and soulless.

Magnus stepped forward, placing the pouch back in his belt, gripping his lance with both hands to confront the stranger. Who is this ... man, general?! he asked, stepping in front of Titus like a shield.

The warrior folded his thick arms across his armor, giving Magnus an utterly fearless smile that revealed unusually sharp incisors among his white teeth.

Titus stepped around Magnus, pressing on his arms to lower his weapon as he
passed. Relax, Magnus, he said. This
splendid beast of destruction is my newest
recruit. One of my couriers managed to
lure him away from his mercenary alliance
with the Scythian Nomads. And as one of
few exceptions to certain ethnos require-
ments, he s now part of a secret *cohort* I m
developing within the Praetorian Guard.

Magnus held his lance to the side,
studying the titan before him. His stature
wasn t the only unnatural trait about him.
His eyes were hidden in small shadows,
defying the light of the general s torch illuminating the rest of his face. His whole
appearance reminded Magnus about the
tales of the evil *gibborim.*

Titus stepped up beside the warrior,
slapping the dark bicep on his right arm
with his introduction. Magnus, I want you
to meet the most relentless and fearless
warrior I have ever come across, present
company excluded, of course, he smiled.
He is the terror known only as Tsavo. I
first heard about him when I was in
Alexandria several years ago.

Magnus stood quietly unimpressed,
his suspicion building as a veil of silence
fell over the small clearing where they
stood.

Titus moved back down between the
two warriors locked in a dead stare with
one another. Wait for me outside the

grove, Tsavo, he ordered. I ll join you in a moment.

Tsavo did not move. There was only the appearance of a fierce scowl on his bullish face to show he was unwilling to yield position.

I said leave us, Tsavo! Titus repeated, his tone rising with authority, eyes dancing royally in the light of his torch.

The giant took in a breath through his large nostrils, releasing it in a slow and indignant manner, lightly rapping the breast of his armor with a fisted salute before walking back to the other side of the grove.

Titus turned to Magnus again. There is no need to feel threatened by Tsavo s presence, Magnus.

I am not threatened in the least, sire.

Then what is it, other than Tsavo s sudden appearance, that unnerves you?

Magnus glanced at the large figure lingering in the shadows on the other side of the grove. There s something about him that I don t trust, general.... Something unnatural.

Titus looked back at the giant. He is a rare feast for the eyes, isn t he? There are wild legends about him that abound throughout Egypt. It s even been said that he s over three thousand years old, and that he is one of the Titans spawned from seed of the gods that hover in the heavens around us.

Magnus squinted at the large silhouette in the distance while listening to Titus tale.

Such stories seem to carry a weight of possibility when you first behold him, don t they? the general noted, glancing back at Magnus with a sardonic grin.

Magnus didn t notice the general s smug demeanor because of his intense focus that was still trained sharply on the giant s darkened silhouette.

Titus stepped in front of him, demanding the warrior s attention with the flames of his torch. Give no more thought to Tsavo this night, Magnus, he ordered. I need you at your best tomorrow when you lead your *cohort* units in support of the first wave against the zealot defenses at the Temple. Crush all who resist you. But do not take the Temple. That is mine to conquer. At this point I don t want it damaged. I feel a certain inclination to preserve it as a trophy to the glory of my father s reign.

Magnus gaze fell towards the ground when he suddenly remembered the significance of what day and month it was. Regardless of Titus desire to capture the House of the Lord intact, he knew the oracles of the Prophet Daniel and the Gospel of Luke concerning the destruction of Zerubbabel s refurbished Temple were on the verge of coming true. Numerically true. For this very night was the eve before the centuries old anniversary of Nebuchadnezzar s destruction of the first Temple.

Do you have a problem with your orders? Titus asked, snapping Magnus from his haunted stare.

Magnus shook his head. No, general.

Good.

Magnus expression became heavier with concern the more he thought about the destruction to come. I will hold you to your word, general, he replied.

My word?

Concerning my wife, he reminded him.

Yes, of course, he said. As I told you, I will do what I can.

Magnus nodded his thanks, still unsure what measure of cooperation his request would truly receive tomorrow in the heat of battle.

There will be a brief conclave with Tiberius and the other commanders of the army in the morning before the assault on the Temple to make a final decision on whether we should destroy it or preserve it, Titus replied. Make sure you have your reserve units at the base of this mountain in place before then.

I will, general.

With that, Titus started to leave, only to stop and face him again with a final word. You re my best officer, Magnus.... I m counting on you to remember your place in the scheme of things tomorrow. I will not fail in this siege of Jerusalem as Cestius Gallus failed in his.

Magnus rapped the breast of his armor with a fisted salute as the Imperial Son turned and hiked back up the slope, Tsavo taking to his side the moment the general exited the grove.

Magnus looked back at Jerusalem again after the general and his strange escort rode away. He sighed in a tired breath, bowing his head against his lance.

Magnus stood on the flat ledge of rock for another hour, lost in the memories of his past while gazing back and forth across the expanse of the city in the vicinity of the Temple area, hoping for some sort of signal from his beloved to tell him that she was still alive. But the distance was just too far for him to bring the house he had inherited from his father into focus.

Distracted, Magnus didn t notice the change in the night s atmosphere. The moon had grown brighter somehow, the sky ripening to a purple hue, teeming with stars shining like stones in a rippling brook.

Magnus began to notice the changes taking place all around him. He was surprised by a shaft of light descending from the sky in front of him, landing on the rocky slope several feet away, concentrating on one spot as it expanded like a circular curtain.

He took a step back on the flat ledge, raising his lance as the heavenly vision swirled majestically before him. The shaft of light rolled for several seconds before dissolving, revealing an enormous figure of a man clothed in a luminous robe of sky-blue flax. Heavy armaments could be seen outlined beneath the stranger s ethereal garment.

Magnus lowered his lance slowly, the Lord s Spirit softening his defenses. The stranger was taller than the giant he had encountered earlier even though he was standing on the slope beneath his ledge of rock.

Who are you? Magnus asked respectfully, trying to see the stranger s face cloaked beneath the robe s large hood.

The stranger walked up to Magnus, looming higher than the warrior without actually standing on the overhanging rock. You re not frightened by my appearance? asked the stranger, his voice like an echo from a deep well.

Magnus was visibly stunned by the stranger s words when he spoke in a tongue never uttered for his hearing before. But somehow he understood. The texture of the language was similar to a form of ancient Hebrew he was taught as a child.

The stranger could see the confusion on Magnus face. I speak in the language first spoken by Adam, he said. You understand it because I speak to what is buried within you.

Magnus confusion melted into awe. He was beginning to understand a measure of what was happening, hoping this stranger before him had come with the answer to his prayers.

Are you not yet frightened by my appearance and strange words? he asked.

Magnus thought for a second before answering. I should be, he answered. I should be on my face as a dead man.... But I am not.

And why is that?

Magnus answered more boldly as the Holy Spirit who lived within him hardened his Adamic frame with the proper strength and response. I have seen God in the flesh. And I fear neither man nor angel. I fear only him. I bow ... only to him.

And that is why I have been sent to you, brave one, he said.

The stranger lifted his hands that looked like bronze-colored glass, each as large as Magnus head. He gripped the sides of his luminous hood, pulling it back slowly to reveal a burnished, man-shaped face chiseled to a stony countenance, accented by disheveled locks of black hair that emanated with a rainbow-colored aura for a few seconds before fading. Solid-blue corneas burned brightly in his eye sockets, shimmering with golden irises and diamond pupils. I am Michael, a servant of the Lord Jesus, the risen Christ, he told him.

Michael? said Magnus, the name ringing with great power and familiarness. You ... are the great prince the Prophet Daniel wrote about.... God s Archangel.

Yes. And I have come to you with an urgent commission from the Most High.

Magnus drove his lance into a cleft in the rock beside his foot. The campaign.... That s why you re here, isn t it?

Michael nodded. This night I must once again stand aside as outside forces in the terrestrial realm seek to destroy the Children of Abraham. The hopes of the zealots for self-rule and the establishment of a new dynasty will be crushed. But Israel s seed will not be obliterated. It will flourish in other nations as it has in the past.

I have no wish to be part of this campaign, Magnus replied. But I have no love for the zealots or their political regime. What happens to them now matters little to me. I only wish for the safety of the innocent. That is what weighs heavily upon me. War shows little mercy to those caught in the middle.

You have seen much during your life here on Earth. And you speak from a heart as large with compassion as it is with valor and loyalty. You have been endowed with a passion which cannot be bound by the words or deeds of other men. That is the reason why I have come to you. It is time for you to inherit the Legacy ordained for you from on high.

I don t understand, Magnus said. I thought you were here to answer my prayer for the safety of those who have nothing to do with the zealot s revolt.

I have always protected those who belong to the Most High, said Michael. But that is not why I have revealed myself to you this night. I am here to coronate you with the holiest of mantles. It was first held by the Anointed Cherub. But it was forsaken when he sought equality with the Lord Most High. His pride and jealousy lured him into a delusional darkness forever. And because of it, he and all those who followed him in his rebellion will one day be confined to the depths of Hell forever.

Michael paused for a moment, lifting his eyes to the stars. But our Lord, in his divine wisdom, would not let that mantle be destroyed with the evil one s rebellion, he continued, looking back down at the warrior. He would shape and hammer the mantle into something new, passing it to the hands of noble men at the appointed time. Moses was the first to inherit it; Joshua would be his heir. It was later passed to the judges of Israel such as Shamgar, Samson and Samuel. King David and his thirty-seven men of valor were next in line.

Magnus stepped back a pace, somewhat daunted by any comparison of himself to Israel s most revered patriarchs. These are great men whom you speak of. But what do they have to do with me?

Michael drew a step closer to the flat rock where Magnus stood. They were each special champions with different powers and mission objectives, he answered. And you have been chosen to continue the Legacy. To be ... the next Shekinah Champion.

Shekinah Champion?

Yes, Michael nodded. A champion of light.... A role you were marked for before you were even born. It was the same with the others.

I don t understand. The Christos One was the ultimate champion. What need is there for another?

You speak with truth and loyalty from the depths of your heart, Magnus. And that is why the Lord delights in passing this holy mantle to you. Michael took another step closer. He desires to see your faith flourish throughout the ages.

And to watch as you discover your destiny as a living foreshadow of the wrath to come.

Wrath?

Yes, Michael replied. You will be a living foreshadow of divine judgments to return in full after the Ascension of the Church.

What about my wife?

Michael placed his hand on Magnus shoulder. Remember our Lord, and hold not to the things of your present life that will become the former.

Magnus bowed his head. The vision of his wife sung to the heart of his youth, whispering the sweet memory of when they first met in Jerusalem s marketplace. But the cries of the Carpenter nailed to the *xulon* tree for his sins quickly overpowered the image, wrapping around his thoughts with the suffocating pitch of his sacrifice. Its embrace was a piercing reminder, resonating in his spirit with Blood-soaked thunder as it cut through the flesh of his own desires. He knew he could deny his Lord nothing.

What does the Lord require of me? he asked as he lifted his head slowly.

Rest easy, Magnus. Your precious Rachel, like the rest of your family, belongs to the Lord. He will always take care of her.

Magnus stared at him. He knew his words were true. But his assurances of her ultimate safety did not vanquish his desire to do what he could to protect her himself.

Michael took a step back and held out his glassy hands, palms facing up. A bronze bowl appeared between his hands in a flash of spiraling flames. Take this, he said. It is Shekinah Wine. A vintage of stored up wrath. It will sustain you for as long as you walk the road of the *Wayfarer Call*.

How long will that be?

It is not for you to know the times and seasons, Magnus.

But....

Take it, he urged. It is your destiny. It is what you were born for.

Magnus took the bronze bowl with both hands, pressing his fingers to some of the fiery-blue symbols of ancient Hebrew etched around the bowl s lip. He rolled the bowl between his fingers, stirring the dark-blue liquid sparkling inside it. The sense of honor and duty instilled since childhood called out to him from his rugged reflection in the wine.

He closed his eyes and inhaled the sweet aroma of the sparkling wine, pressing his lower lip against one of the sets of flaming symbols near the bowl s rim representing the gematria of 999. The liquid rushed over his tongue with a taste as rapturous as the fruit, exploding with a powerful jolt of electricity while making its way down his throat in one long gulp, coursing throughout his entire body in a matter of seconds. The bowl disappeared in a flash of spiraling flames as the sudden jolt of added power brought him to his knees in a clap of thunder. The wine s Edenic enzymes surged throughout his body, their chemical reactions instantly enlarging his lung capacity and blood flow, fortifying his immune system with a stalwart shield against human disease.

Magnus rocked backwards where he had fallen, arms outstretched, mouth gaping slightly at the sight of the moon and stars growing brighter with each passing second. The mountain s olive trees loomed over him, sentry-like. Another fiery sensation electrified his skeleton while he peered at the strange anomalies around him, his back arcing in a sharp snap from the shock of his flesh and bones hardening to a preternatural density. Thousands of pin needles of light danced across the surfaces of his emerald eyes simultaneously, pulsing up and down. The heavens burned with fire as the needles of light parted at the center of each eye, dissolving away as the Holy Spirit who lived within him allowed the Shekinah Subconsciousness of his mind to roll back the veil to the spirit world like a scroll.

Michael placed his right foot on the ledge of rock and leaned into the champion s line of sight, resting his hand in the center of his *lorica* armor.

Magnus could see countless winged beings stretched out against the field of stars behind Michael s head, with horseless, fiery-wheeled chariots and siege ships of the strangest design streaking by beneath them while they made a slow descent from the sky.

Rise, Magnus.

The champion focused on the Archangel s ethereal eyes at the sound of his deep voice, his mind teeming with increased brain activity.

Michael offered a hand to help him to his feet.

Another small clap of thunder rolled through the air as Magnus slapped the Archangel s forearm with a hearty embrace of his hand, feeling as though he could catapult himself over the city below from the immense power flowing through him.

Magnus released the Archangel s forearm, taking a step back, staring at his right hand with a look of awe, feeling the added power from on high flowing through his veins like a fiery flood. The aches and pains of his impressive mortal frame acquired from a life of endless training and military campaigns were gone. To be twenty-five again would not compare by any measure to the sensation of the wine that now consumed him.

He looked up at Michael. This is incredible, he remarked with a shrug of his shoulders. I can hardly feel the weight of my armaments.... I feel almost naked.

The power of the Shekinah Wine has bonded with your blood, Michael replied. Your human limitations in this realm are almost nonexistent now. And the fighting skills you mastered in your *probatio* training and the *hippika gymnasia* have been amplified a thousand times over.

Magnus thought about the ramifications of inheriting such strength and skill. This cannot be good, he said, holding both hands in front of him. This is too much. This kind of power could make a man feel like ... a god.

Michael placed his foot back on the lower slope again. But you are not a god, he noted. You have simply received a greater portion of power from above just as Elisha did when he inherited Elijah s mantle. Your fear of the one true God, and the fact that the Holy Spirit dwells within you, will help keep you in line with your calling like Moses and the others before you. Always remember the source of the power given to you when you re tempted to believe more of yourself than you should.

I will.

Magnus moved to get a better look at the new picture of Jerusalem burning brightly behind the Archangel. I can see you re not alone, he said, pointing at the wingless angels hovering above the city in fiery ranks.

No, I m not, he answered, turning towards the city.

Magnus peered up at the darker angels with the glowing eyes and the strange siege ships spread across the upper atmosphere of the surrounding mountains. Then they belong to the evil one.

Yes.

They re as fierce-looking as I ve always imagined them to be.... Every bit the monsters haunting the shadows of my childhood.

Michael turned back around with a nod of his head. Your knowledge of the Scriptures serves you well. And that knowledge, with the Holy Spirit s guid-ance, will enhance greatly as you continue to study the Word. You will....

A sudden chorus of crickets dis-tracted Magnus from the Archangel s instruction, echoing loudly in his ears from the grove of trees behind him. My ears.... The sounds of the night are like thunder, he marveled.

It s one of the many changes your body has undergone, he explained. Your skin and the density of your bones have already hardened to a preternatural state. And your eyes will forever glow like coals of emerald fire in the shadows. It s an effect similar to the Shekinah Glory that shone on Moses face when it wasn t veiled. But the powers you have yet to discover will be the most extraordinary effects of the wine you will experience.

Such as?

With a simple thought, you can soar through the air with angelic speed, he started. Your strength is as great as twenty of my best warriors, if not more. And the only things that can draw your blood are weapons and flames of preternatural design. But rest assured, no mortal weapon in this age, or the ages to come, can harm you. The hottest of mortal flames and the coldest of environments cannot touch your life, either. But you can still feel their bite to a tolerable amount. Your clothing will have a measure of protection from impacts and forces of speed applied to them by the Shekinah Wine that feeds the energy stored up in the ionic bonds of sodium in your skin.

Michael paused for a moment, conveying a sense of caution with his piercing stare into Magnus bright eyes. And be sure to guard the level of your voice, he warned. For it is now the *Sword of the Lord*. At its top pitch, you can cause an earth-shattering shockwave that will devastate everything before you for as far as the scope of your eyes can behold, including the rebel hosts of the evil one. Its power is harnessed and unleashed according to the content of your targeting thoughts. So beware.

Magnus touched his lips lightly with his fingers at such a warning. I will be careful, he said softly.

In time, you will learn to master the range of these powers. For they are powers that do have limits as the Holy Spirit will teach you.

Magnus nodded, desiring to explore his powers. I want to fly! he exclaimed, looking down with wonder to see his spiked boots beginning to lift off the rock before even voicing his desire.

He rose slowly, floating breathlessly above Michael s head with outstretched arms. He ascended faster with a thought, the wind rushing against his dark head, his purple-hooded cloak flapping wildly behind him. He spun around in a corkscrew motion, the mountainside twisting below as he rose above the tops of the trees. He stopped in mid-twirl above one of the trees bordering the grove, the top branch brushing against the spiked soles of his cavalry boots.

The bones of his body felt bloated with air while hovering in place, smiling like a child. He peered out across the landscape, noting the hosts in the distance positioned rank and file above Jerusalem, oblivious to any care he had for the moment.

The pull of Michael s voice snapped him from his sudden rapture. Come down, Magnus, he called.

Magnus twirled around and projected himself backwards, arms and cloak shooting over his head as he dropped like a stone. Flying had become second nature to him in a matter of seconds, controlling his descent with subconscious ease.

At the last moment before impact, Magnus slowed the rate of his fall, floating down gently on the ledge in front of Michael. I love this feeling! It s majestic.

It does have a limitation, though, said the Archangel. You cannot ascend past breathing level. Though you could hold your breath for an inordinate amount of time, the lack of air in the upper atmosphere would eventually render you unconscious.

What are my other limits?

Michael rolled his wide shoulders. You must remember that you have been gifted with a tremendous power, to see and hear the activities in the realm of the spirit. You can touch this realm and bring judgment where the Holy Spirit leads. But it can touch you as well, he pointed. Which will be to your advantage at times.

It will?

Yes, he said. Physical matter can affect angels when we re engaged in combat. Even though the atomic sparks of life that make up the structural substance of our spiritual bodies are filled with a great deal of empty space that can be manipulated, it is sometimes difficult for us to pass through solid objects once our minds are locked in a heated battle. That will be a great equalizer for you since you are unable to move through solid objects at any time in your present state.

Why is that not one of my powers?

Because you haven t been glorified yet, he answered. Your body has great power and is impervious to the weapons of man, but it is not the same as the Shekinah Body that our Lord had at his resurrection. You will inherit that glorified state when the *Trumpet of the Lord* heralds the Ascension of the Church.

Michael drew closer to Magnus. The evil one and his forces will oppose you with great prejudice, he continued. They re powerful. And they re not to be underestimated. They have created a vast empire in the first and second heavens known as the Outer Realm, as well as the *cosmos* systems of human government that dominate this planet. It is a dominion allotted a time of sufferance until their cup of wickedness is full. And because of it, you will always be behind enemy lines. Never let the illusions of physical might blind you to that.

Magnus nodded silently, listening to every word carefully as if he were a teenager again in the *probatio* training camps being taught his first lesson in the art of war.

You must take guard against the mercenary *gibborim* of the evil one, Michael further warned, especially the one called Tsavo. He s a shapeshifter.... The last of the original giants from the second wave of Nephilimite Conquerors spawned by rebel angels after the age of the Antediluvian World. And though he is a champion of the fallen ones, his sole desire is to wear the *Covenant Harness*; a beastly headdress with a mantle of flexible armor that was shaped by the hands of the evil one himself after the decline of Nimrod s empire. It is promised to the one known as the Great Tree who will rule over the kingdoms of the *latter days*.

Michael took note of the enemy ranks still making their slow descent from the heights of the upper atmosphere. This armor was placed in the care of an *ashshaph* from the Order of Tammuz in the land of Shinar, he went on, looking back down at Magnus. The sorcerer was charged with protecting the *Covenant Harness* from pretenders to the throne. To help with this task, he formed a secret brotherhood of *chakhamim* warriors known as the Harness Magi to help protect the mantle throughout the centuries from mercenaries like Tsavo. But the giant s knowledge of the covenant mantle has made him desperate to prove he alone is worthy to rule over the kingdoms of men. His taste for blood and power is insatiable. So beware.

Magnus nodded, giving place in his mind to the vision of the bull-like warrior. By what means can he be destroyed?

Though ancient power flows through him, he is not indestructible, he answered. You can destroy him by way of drowning or the taking of his head as David did with Goliath.

Magnus thought for a moment, imagining what it would be like to go hand-to-hand with the giant as David had done with the mighty Goliath.

Michael drew even closer, his face and eyes burning with purity. At the appointed time, you must seek out the iron sarcophagus of King Og of Bashan. The Holy Spirit will lead you. In it, you will find a weapon of adamantine lore. It was a blade once held by Goliath, to be used against the Israelites. But it was captured by David when he defeated the giant in the Valley of Elah, only to be secretly placed back in Og s tomb after the Shepherd King s death. Use only the knowledge of its riddle in the shaping of your own weapons of war. But remember this.... Blood-stained spikes are the keys to unlocking the greatest power you have.

Michael placed his large hands on the warrior s shoulders. Use all your powers to defend those who are weak, he urged.

Go where the Spirit of the Lord leads you. Preach the Gospel and administer judgment where God demands it. But be careful about revealing your powers to others. Misdirection will help keep the enemy at bay. And a degree of anonymity will be health to your bones.

Magnus nodded silently.

A final word of warning to you, champion. No matter what you see in the light of the day to come, do not interfere with the campaign against the zealots.... The Temple will be destroyed, and many will be scattered.

Michael noticed the champion s eyes trembling with a lover s fear. Hear me, Magnus, he said. The horrors of this world and the effects of the *Wayfarer Call* will tempt the emotions of your Adamic nature like never before....

Michael stepped back from the champion with that warning, reaching behind his neck with both hands to pull the hood of his luminous robe back over his head. But fear not, you beloved son of *The Way*. The Lord is with you always, even unto the end of the age.

Magnus stood silent, watching the Archangel turn and retreat along the mountain s rocky slope. Michael, wait. What about my wife? What will become of Rachel?

Before Magnus could move, Michael was consumed in a fiery blaze, shooting into the sky like a blue comet. The Archangel cut a bright path through the heavens, disappearing through the ranks of rebel hosts descending from above in a rumbling flash of light.

Magnus searched the units of horse-less chariots and siege ships speeding back and forth in the upper atmosphere, bringing the images of the rebels closer with a simple, concentrated thought. The faces of the rebels were of differing shapes, but similar to the veneers of men. Their eyes were completely black except for their irises that were shaped like five-pointed stars, each rotating counterclock-wise in the center of their orbs, glowing like red and yellow suns.

Lightning flashes from drawn swords and exposed fangs suddenly filled the spectrum of his magnified vision.

Magnus struggled to find any trace of Michael in the descending ranks of evil, clenching his fists in frustration.

Michael, he called out again, careful to control the power of his voice. Come back!

Magnus shot up into the air suddenly, the wind rushing hard against his bronze face. The sight of the descending ranks mattered nothing to him at the moment, Mount Scopus quickly becoming a distant speck beneath him. Michael s earlier warn-ings about flying too high went unheeded. His breaths quickly became strained when he neared the strange chariots of the descending horde, eyes draining of their moisture as a spell of dizziness started to set in, lungs constricting.

Michael, he called, his voice muffled by the thin veil of oxygen. He could see nothing but the fiery wheels of the chariots and the countless eyes of glowing menace that consumed the positions of the stars. The frigid winds of the rebels showered him from above in a stinging mist, bringing him to a stifled hover.

Magnus turned as the chariots sped by him in lightning intervals, rotating wildly, the frigid vapors from above becoming thicker, mixing with his exhausted breaths. Chaos filled his mind. Never had he seen such evil wonders before. Horseless chariots and siege ships blew by on each side of him like infernal cavalry, the howls of rebel angels thundering with blasphemy and contempt in his ears.

His head slumped forward as the thundering chaos and the frigid mist from above caused him to black out, severing the power holding him in the air. He fell backwards between the speeding chariots, arms and legs flailing about while he plummeted toward the ground, the wind swishing and slicing around him in furious wails.

Mount Scopus thundered softly as Magnus crashed to the spot where the

Archangel had been standing only moments ago, sending clouds of dirt and jagged debris flying high into the air as his hardened frame created a deep crater on impact. The large slab of rock where he had been standing earlier broke off from the mountainside and shifted down the slope from the force of his crash, with several trees from the surrounding grove following. The large slab slid over the mouth of the crater, sealing Magnus in the Earth.

———

Beams of sunlight peaked through the cracks around the oblong-shaped slab of rock covering the crater s mouth. Magnus shifted his head when he felt the warmth of the sun prick his fingertips that rested near the upper edges of the crater s interior. A burning aroma seeped in with the small beams of sunlight as well, swirling around his nose with the dust he stirred by the slow movements of his arms.

Magnus started to shift the rest of his body beneath the slab, his senses awakening to the burning smell seeping into his shallow tomb. He lifted his hand flat against the belly of the slab, sliding the ton-heavy rock to the right with an unconscious ease, the full force of the sun hitting him in the face. His bright eyes quickly resumed their normal color in the daylight.

He could tell it was well past the fifth hour of the day from the sun s descent towards the west. A single name gripped his thoughts suddenly as a hot wind swept across the mountainside where he lay, slicing over his exposed face in a smoky stench.

Rachel, he muttered, her name quivering off his lips as the scent of smoldering flesh filled the air.

Magnus sat up quickly. His eyes fell on a merciless display of impaled bodies that had doubled in number on each side of the city s northern road. Flames and blustering clouds of smoky ruin soiled the sky above the walled province beyond the groves of torture. The Scorpion catapults once used to launch showers of iron-tipped darts were abandoned in front of the siege banks. Black plumes of smoke circled the towers of the Antonia Fortress as Zerubbabel s refurbished Temple burned uncontrollably, the fire having spread throughout its intersecting structures and the columned pavilion of the Royal Stoa on the southern wall of the Temple Mount.

Magnus sprang to the rim of the crater with a quick push of his hands, ripping his ragged cloak from around his neck as he landed on the slope. Rachel!

He vaulted forward with another quick leap, cutting a high arc through the air before landing back down on the mountainside again, his mind taking quick action to control the adrenaline mixing with the heavenly wine coursing through his veins. He drew his spatha blade in his dash down the steep slope, swinging it like it was a natural extension of his hand while leaping over craggy outcroppings with the ease of a deer. The landscape around him blurred in his race through the groves of tree stumps where mighty palm, olive and myrtle trees had once populated the lower sides of Mount Scopus.

A trail of dust followed as he crossed the Kidron Valley at the foot of Lookout Hill in a matter of seconds.

Magnus speed slowed to a normal pace almost immediately when he reached the northern road where the first zealots were impaled, the wall of dust behind him subsiding.

The rawest stench of death and bile-layered decay descended on him in a heavy cloud at his entry into the pathway of dead and dying zealots. Roman soldiers standing at the bases of the wooden pales recognized Rome s most decorated Prae-fecti walking into their grove of torments, talking in hushed voices with one another while he passed in front of them.

Magnus stopped in the middle of the pathway, staring up to his right at a hag-gard, torn face of a young zealot hanging in the familiar pose of impalement, wrists spiked through on the sides of his rood just above his head, feet doubled over and fastened in similar fashion. Needles of

light pulsed across the champion s eyes
suddenly as his mind subconsciously tore
back the veil of the spirit world. A hulking
apparition appeared on top of the pale
above the zealot s head in the form of
watery flames rolling outward like a scroll,
the split fire vanishing in small plumes of
light as the formidable shape of a rebel
angel became more defined. Black eyes of
rotating fire stared back at him from the
top of the rood, their glow shining through
tresses of long hair framing the sides of
the rebel s predatory face. An infernal
crossbow hung from the right side of the
armored apron fastened around his waist,
with a sickle sword hanging on the left. A
round black shield was attached to his left
arm, with gold, antiquarian markings of
angelic origin inscribed on its rolled-out
center to signify his membership in the
Nekros Order; an elite group of rebel hosts
specializing in the art of search and
destroy.

The rebel flashed his sharp, iron-like
teeth at the champion with a sneer of
laughter, the bottom tips of his wings billowing with motion on each side of the
zealot s head hanging beneath his perch,
looking as though they weren t natural
appendages, but rather illusions of
assumption.

A cold chill swept over Magnus body
as thousands of similarly-armed rebels
materialized on each side of the road,

perched in identical crouching positions above the heads of the impaled zealots, their strange wings billowing outward from the tops of the pales like black banners.

He watched as more fallen angels burned into view. The fiery chariots and the siege ships from last night filled the sky in rings of spaced-out regiments, stretching like a hovering net across the airspace of the entire city. There was no sign of Michael or his warriors anywhere as pillars of black smoke continued to climb high above the city walls. The sounds of war and human agony spreading over the groves of the executed in thick clouds of ruin, eclipsing the sun in smoky intervals. He felt utterly alone, stranded at the mouth of a hell on Earth. Michael s words that he would always be behind enemy echoed through his feverish mind as sporadic flakes of human ash and city debris began to rain down on him.

Magnus was unable to mourn the city of his Jewish heritage. His thoughts were fixed on his wife, and the promise Titus had made to him. But his failure to show up and lead his men in the final assault on the zealots would have consequences. His fear was not for himself, however. He had been called to a higher purpose; no man could strike a death blow against him now. Few had come close to doing so even before his induction into the Shekinah

Legacy last night. But that was not true for the ones he loved.

He quickly started forward, splintering the ivory hilt of his spatha sword with an increased grip, beads of cold sweat rolling down his face. His eyes searched left and right, keeping watch for the slightest movement from the rebel angels or the soldiers on either side of the road.

The champion walked for what seemed like hours, listening to the hushed voices of the soldiers ringing clear in his powerful ears through all the weakened moans of the impaled.

The pitch of the war reached its peak for Magnus as he rounded a bend in the road, walking into the shadow of a ten-foot rood planted in front of the northern gateway s blackened arch. The sword fell from his hands, tears flooding his eyes at the sight of his wife hanging in a broken pose above him, smoke and flames ascending behind her on the other side of the blackened gateway. Rachel s arms were stretched above her head and nailed to the sides of the pale. Her black hair masked the sides of her head which dangled toward a familiar sword lodged deep in her chest. The blood ran thick along the blade and ornate hilt of Titus parazonium blade, soaking her fringed dress as it dripped heavily over her knees.

The rebels perched on top of the other pales roared like ravenous wolves when Magnus fell against the roods knotted trunk.

He dug his fingers into the dead tree beneath his wifes feet, the tears blurring his vision as he splintered and cracked the knotted wood with his hands, snapping the trunks base in half while the demons roared triumphantly behind him. He caught the transplanted tree in its teeter to the left, gently wrapping his left arm around Rachels body while laying the broken trunk on the ground. He pulled the spikes from her wrists carefully, casting them aside. He then removed the blade from her chest in the same manner and flung it behind him.

Magnus knelt beside her body, pulling her to his chest, stroking the hair away from her face that was matted with blood and dirt, the glory of her raven-like mane tarnished forever. The moment he had feared most and prayed vehemently against since the beginning of the siege had come true. Brutally true.

He could only stare at her broken body in disbelief. Even in his worst nightmares, he never imagined she would suffer such a death. She was the flesh now stripped from his bones; one of the tenderest blooms of life and human love he would ever know.

Avenge her, young one, a cold voice said from above. Avenge her with all the power at your disposal.

Magnus looked up through his tears, feeling the blackest depths of despair creep over his soul. A golden-haired rebel with metallic, crimson-colored wings encrusted with carved feathers, jeweled eyes and silver symbols stood before him. His golden eyes were those of a dragon, with black, six-pointed stars rotating in different directions in the fang-like irises of crimson fire burning in the center of each eye.

Avenge her, the rebel repeated, his frigid voice echoing in the champions mind rather than his ears. Claim your legal rights of vengeance, young champion.... Claim them!

The moment was quicker than the eye as the mysterious rebel vanished in a hot wind of dust and smoke-layered shadow, his unspoken invitations swirling around him in fading whispers and vapors of stringed music.

Magnus stood to his feet without a word, his mind overwhelmed with confusion and despair. The howls of the rebels subsided into sharp snickers as he turned around from the blackened gateway and started to walk away, his wife cradled in his arms, tears rolling down his face.

The taunts of the rood-perched rebels and the murmurings of the Roman soldiers standing below them faded to mere echoes as Magnus walked along the road. His tears fell onto Rachel s face, mingling with the flakes of ash raining down on them.

A small contingent of the rebels exploded off some of the pales on the left side of the road when a scarlet-colored power from the Council of Thrones hierarchy swept down from the sky, following the champion from a distance.

Magnus fell to his knees at the foot of Mount Scopus, defeated, kneeling beside a shallow grave dug with his own hands. He was holding Rachel in his arms, stroking her raven-colored hair. She was a pale reflection of her former beauty, her brown skin sullied and tortured at the hands of men he thought he could trust; the words of Vespasian s son ringing with a hollow resonance in his mind.

His emerald eyes clouded as he thought of the impoverished life she had lived before they met. She had been abandoned as a child, forced to survive among beggars and lepers scrounging for food left over in the fields of wheat merchants. She was nearly half his age when they first met in Jerusalem s marketplace. But the attraction was instant. Her beauty had caused great commotion in the marketplace that day as her guardian, an unscrupulous merchant, put her on the auction block. He remembered the fierce bidding, the highest offers coming from the caravan of an

Ethiopian prince. But he quickly trumped the prince s offer, doubling the bid to the crowd s great astonishment. The merchant refused to believe that Magnus, a Roman officer, was able to pay such a price. But when he revealed the seal of his mother s house, the deal was quickly closed. Rachel responded with tears and surprise, not knowing what to expect from a master who would pay so much for one with as seemingly little value as she. Her biggest surprise came later when she was set free. In addition, he had given her double the fortune paid for her, making sure she would be taken care of for the rest of her life. They wed a year later, two years before the beginning of the Jewish War.

Magnus pulled her to his chest. He closed his eyes and kissed her blood-dried lips tenderly, the sweetness of their fruit having faded. Holy Father, he whispered against her mouth, please bring her back to me.... Please, Father, restore her.... Please, Father!

Silence was the only reply from Heaven.

The champion leaned forward and placed her body in the grave. He then looked upward with pleading eyes, placing his hands on the wound in her chest as if to allow the immense power already flowing through him to be God s instrument to raise her. Tragically, such powers of resurrection and healing, like those given to the

Apostles for the testimony of authenticity, would not be found amongst the arsenal at his disposal.

Magnus sobbed softly at the continued silence from above, his bloodied hands trembling against her chest as he waited for the miracle he knew deep within him would not come.

Time seemed to stand still until he reluctantly pulled back his hands. At that moment a shadow fell over his face from the bowing of his head, the tears drying against his face in the heat of a building rage. His own heart thundered in his ears with thoughts of tearing Titus limb from limb, a power that did reside within him.

Yessss, a voice hissed from behind. Destroy him, champion.

Magnus opened his eyes with a bright and hateful glare, slowly rising to his feet. His demeanor hardened when he turned and came face to face with a towering angel. The scarlet-colored rebel was a mountain of sleek muscle that shimmered like Morganite stone, his deceptive wings rustling through the air behind him, the tips of his oil-dark hair looped with golden rings. The black eyes of his humanoid face blazed with star-shaped irises of yellow fire rotating in counterclockwise patterns, fangs emerging in a jester s smile. A scale-armored apron with a sickle sword on one side and a preternatural crossbow on the other was fastened around his waist beneath a muscled breastplate of black adamantine, with a miniature, jewel-marked shield of gold nestled between the breastplate s pectorals; its markings signifying his authority over the Nekros Order.

Leave me, spirit, Magnus growled, his fiery eyes piercing the other warriors hovering in the air behind the lead rebel in a submissive silence.

A Shekinah Champion for only one day, and already you speak with season.

Leave me! he repeated.

Very well. I will leave you to your anger. The rebel leaned close to Magnus face, his black eyes flush with the heat of rotating stars. Do your worst, champion.... Do your worst.

The rebel drew back in a windswept fluster of wings, rising backward into the air amongst the Nekros warriors with howls of spiteful laughter. The motley crew streaked across the sky in a wide arc, descending toward the chaos still bubbling at the heart of the ancient city.

A cloud of dust rose from the road of the impaled zealots beneath the band of retreating rebels, marking the approach of a small unit of horsemen.

Magnus focused on the cloud with a vengeful scowl, clenching his fists, hardening his stance in front of his wife s grave, her blood dripping through his tightened fingers, echoing in his ears with each splatter on the ground.

The cloud of dust faded as sixteen of his own men from the horse-archer *cohorts* thundered to a halt some twenty feet away. Armed with javelins, they moved to surround him.

Magnus eyes settled on the one who led them, watching as Titus himself positioned his familiar mount in the middle of the unit s circling formation, barring Magnus path. But he had no intention of running from this confrontation.

Titus dismounted and strode toward Magnus with a certain swagger, casting a military issue writing slat made of wood and a set of iron shackles at his feet.

Magnus looked down at the shackles first before glancing over at the familiar, veneer-thin slat of folded wood. A stylus-tooled depiction of his father s royal seal was positioned beneath the knot of the cord tied around the slat, with a half broken clay replica of the seal s lion s head lumped on top of it.

One of my spies intercepted the secret message you sent to your wife prior to the siege, Titus revealed. And as you know, I am quite fluent in both Greek and Aramaic. I had hoped to orchestrate your downfall in front of my other officers once the city fell. But it seems your cowardly absence has given me the opportunity to destroy you in front of those who truly adored you: your very own men.

Magnus lifted his head with a smoldering stare. You murdered ... my wife, he said lowly, gritting his teeth.

Yes.... Yes, I did, he replied with relish. She s been in my custody all along. But it wasn t until today that I was able to hear her scream for mercy.

Magnus held his ground, the inner rage building to a fever pitch.

Titus drew dangerously close to the champion, squinting with disdain. I always suspected that your loyalties were divided when I found out you had been allowed to keep from taking the mark of the empire. You re as much a barbarian as those zealots who foolishly set those fires in the inner court of the Temple. And I have tolerated your presence in my army because of my father s friendship with the House of Octavius. But no more. I have found the nail to pin your hide to the wall, he sneered, poking his finger against the chest of Magnus scale armor. All I needed was patience, and to watch for treason. Your days of usurping the son of Vespasian are finished!

Titus swung his left hand to the side, striking Magnus on the jaw with a quick backfist in to humiliate him even more with a show of his own strength. The champion s head didn t move, though, as the general grunted in a painful grimace from the hearty blow. It was like striking the side of a marble pillar.

Magnus grabbed Titus offending hand, his movement too fast for the general to see. He crushed it with a simple squeeze, filling the air with the sound of cracking bones.

Titus fell to his knees, screaming in torment.

The archers took aim at their former commander without hesitation, hurling their javelins with great speed and strength, striking Magnus in the arms and back in perfect unison. Each javelin buckled into splinters against the champion s hardened frame, their impacts merely chipping off some of the scales of his armor as the broken weapons bounced off of him.

The archers gazed at one another in disbelief.

Magnus continued to squeeze while Titus writhed in pain at his feet, his wife s blood running through his fingers down along the general s arm. The murderer of my earthly father and brother found mercy in Caligula s exile of him years ago.... But you will find no such quarter with me, he said with finality. To torments I send you!

Magnus drew back his other hand that was tightly drawn into an unforgiving fist.

A force of immense strength caught Magnus arm before he could deliver the blow to the general s head. No! com- manded a voice from behind.

Magnus glared over his left shoulder to see Michael holding his wrist, still clothed in the luminous robe from the night before. You said she would be taken care of, Michael! he cried, pulling the Archangel forward a step with his attempt to jerk his arm free.

Michael increased his grip, looking almost surprised by the raw power flowing through the arm of the new champion. No, Magnus! he repeated. His life is not yours to take! Vengeance belongs to the Lord!

Magnus glared down at Titus, refus- ing to relinquish his hold on him. He looked around at the paralyzed archers on their mounts, confusedly watching the strange scene, glancing back and forth at one another as they each wondered who would dare to make the first move to help their general. They were all more than accustomed to Rome s frequent changes of power in the last few years, and it was always important to make sure you were standing on the right side when the smoke cleared.

Let go of him, Magnus! Michael repeated.

Magnus looked back at the Archangel just at the moment the voice of the Holy Spirit whispered to his heart. *Obey*, said the Lord.

The urging of the Holy Spirit spoke of Rachel s home with the Father above as well, reminding him, too, of how his Savior suffered at the hands of unjust men without striking back with the fullness of divine power.

He let go of Titus hand, tossing the Imperial Son backwards in the process.

Michael released his hold on Magnus and vanished once more.

Titus crawled to his right, pulling himself up by the ankle of one of the archers, tucking his broken hand beneath his arm. Bind him! he panted, falling against the horse s side.

The archer steadied his horse as Titus fell against him, looking to his comrades for help. None of the other archers seemed willing, each reining their steeds backwards several paces.

Magnus felt the cold sting of his loss making one last stab at his broken heart, faint tears hardening in his emerald eyes with his gaze heavenward, the rage of it all exploding through his quivering mouth. FATHER!!!! he shouted, Michael s warning s from the previous night getting lost in the cloud of his emotions as the *Sword of the Lord* was unleashed.

The ground around Magnus feet collapsed into a five-foot crater forty feet in circumference as the shout exploded from his mouth in a seismic wave, rippling like a watery, funnel-shaped explosion. The wave widened when Magnus lowered his head in the motion of the collapsing ground, just missing Titus and the others as the shockwave gathered a rolling wall of sand and other debris in its earth-shattering course.

The rebel angels that were still perched on top of the roods in the distance vaulted into flight as the roaring wave raced toward them, its power cutting the groves of impaled zealots in half, tossing debris in every direction. The wave shifted upward suddenly before striking what was left of the battered city, pulled to a new course by the unseen Will of Heaven which caused the hovering chariots and siege ships to break from their formations. It rushed through the air above the smoking remains of the city, catching some of the rebel hosts by surprise while they sped back and forth across the rooftops in their evil pursuits. Black explosions pulsed throughout the wave as its razor-sharp pressure tore rebel angels in half, their remains falling into a swirling portal to the Abyss that opened in the ground in the center of the city below.

The wave eventually melted away into the horizon.

The air at the foot of Mount Scopus was calm. Magnus was still on his feet in the center of the crater. Titus and his men lay scattered all around him, their frightened horses stirring together in a small herd off to the left.

Titus managed to pull himself to the top of the crater, standing, gazing incredulously at the splintered pales scattered across the landscape in the distance, the bodies of the zealots jumbled together in mounds of flesh and wood.

Titus steadied himself the best he could, tucking his injured hand beneath his other arm as he turned back briskly. On your feet! he shouted to his men who lay dazed and sprawled out in the crater. Show your allegiance to the masters of Rome, and bind this traitor!

Magnus was horrified at what he saw above the rim of the crater, ignoring the general s orders to have him bound. He touched his lips with trembling fingers where miniature, raised symbols in Hebrew burned with an ember s glow to spell out the gematria phrase, *My Wrath*, before eventually sinking into his flesh again. He could only imagine the full destruction that could have been wrought had the Lord not obviously intervened.

He turned around with a sudden thought, finding his wife s grave completely submerged beneath the crater s wall of sand and dirt.

The words of the Lord came to him again. *Obey and submit, my son.*

Magnus swayed at the words while staring at the spot where he had dug his wife s grave, dropping to the sand on his knees at the divine command.

The archers slowly stood to their feet as Titus continued to rant above them.

He doesn t breathe fire! Titus shouted. You ve seen sand storms and earthquakes rise up suddenly before!

The archers glanced at one another, unsure of what to believe.

I said bind him! Titus repeated.

One of the archers grabbed the shackles that were partially covered with sand and dirt at the center of the crater behind Magnus. The other men each drew a second javelin from their side hanging quivers, shoring up their lingering superstitions with a well-trained posture to shock the champion with impalement should he resist. The archer with the iron bands placed them around the wrists of his former Praefecti nervously, trying not to look him in the eye in the process. He then pulled him to his feet with an easy jerk, turning him around to bind his ankles with the other set of shackles that were connected to the wrist bands by a hanging chain.

Titus walked back down into the crater and stood in front of the bound champion, smiling victoriously while endeavoring to hide the pain in his hand. I may have not been able to capture the

Jewish Temple intact as a trophy for my father, but you can be sure of this one promise that I make to you now, brave prince, he sneered, mocking him with Josephus words from the previous night. Your slow destruction will be my prize as your name is blotted out of every book and pillar that recorded your fame. Others will be honored for your ... noble deeds. History will never know you even existed.

Titus drew closer to his bowed head, reaching out towards him with a renewed boldness as he snatched the pouch of silver from Magnus belt. This is all that you have left in this world, he said maliciously. Tutorial reminders of the lesson you didn t learn about the price of cowardice and betrayal. You can ponder their weight as you spend the rest of your life in chains.... Exiled on the Isle of Patmos.

———

Magnus lay sprawled on his back in a deep sleep on a wooden bench in the belly of a Roman slave galley, stripped of his armor and rank. His face and chest were covered in sweat, arms and legs hanging down toward the hull floor, bound by chains that could have been crushed into powder at any time he so desired. A lantern swung back and forth above him, its motion flowing with the galley as it rolled on the sea in a fierce storm, stirring the damp, nauseating cloud of decay permeating the holding quarters from all the bodies of the other slaves that lay dead and dying in the shadows around him. The stench of death, rather than the chains binding him, had kept him flat on his back, sitting heavily on his chest like an abysmal reminder of the blood and carnage of the past few days that had changed his life forever.

Memories and chains were all that remained now. Power from on high to exact complete vengeance rested within him. But it had been surrendered to men of low estate. Men of evil design whose form and skill had touched the shores of his life once again, exacting an even greater price than the one he had paid as a boy born to a royal house with Herodian adversaries.

A scene of strange images emerged in his mind while he slept. He could see himself standing on a moonlit crest of a rocky hill overlooking a beach of burnt clay being assaulted by heavy surf. Blood and water dripped from the tips of his hair, pelting his sleeveless, thigh-length armor of large, signet-like seals of gold rolled up on the sides like lumps of pressed clay, inscribed with bronze symbols of Hebrew in their flat centers beneath the lumped borders of each thickly-hammered seal. The armor was fastened together by a seam of crown-engraved buckles of refined silver arranged single file down the middle of the flexible garment rather than

the side like the *lorica squamata* arma-
ment he was accustomed to wearing. A
helmet partially made of bronze was
tucked under his left arm, with emblems
and a ceremonial face mask cast in a heavenly color of gold. A slightly curved, sin-
gle-edged blade was strapped around his
waist. To crown it all was a leather, crimson-colored cloak with golden emblems
that was draped over his shoulders, its liquid hem swirling around the lion claws
looped around the tops of his boots.

Magnus grasped three Blood-stained
spikes between the fingers of his right fist,
watching the stony ground in front of him
yawn with a thunderous cracking noise.
The granite opened in a counterclockwise
motion as if the rocks were turning to liquid. A blast of black smoke bellowed from
the pit which hardened to a six foot diameter. A large paw rose up over the jagged
rim of the opening, followed by another
one as they each clamped down on the
stony sides of the pit explosively. An enormous, black griffin with red wings
emerged slowly through the pit s swirling
thicket of smoke, hunching its muscular
shoulders forward in a crouching position,
its golden eyes shining with the shape and
power of a dragon. An iron chain hung
around its neck that had a diverse display
of beastly body parts dangling from the
chain s thick links. The winged lion
growled at the champion with an old

hatred as familiar shekels of silver dripped from its fanged jaws, splattering in the blood that was bubbling up from beneath the rocks where the beast was crouched.

Magnus showed no fear of the beast as another entity ascended through the smoke of the pit. The spirit of a beautiful woman decked in precious jewels and seductive garments of purple floated up behind the growling beast. She held a wicker ephah in her hands, and had a dragon-twined cross branded on her forehead with the words *Mother of Harlots* written in Akkadian above it. The word *harlot* was also inscribed on the lead covering that sealed the basket she was holding. But the inscription was written in Hebrew instead of Akkadian, crowning the other engraving in the center of the lead cover that depicted two, stork-winged goddesses carrying an ephah like the spirit woman before him.

His gaze traveled down the slope of the hill where he was standing as the images before him faded into ashy currents of wind, drawn to the waves crashing violently on the beach of burnt clay below. The great sea exploded in front of him as a black and red dragon with two heads ascended through the surface in a funnel of water, its crimson-colored wings arcing high above each head, shimmering with ancient symbols, jewels and eagle-style feathers that were carved like worked metal between the vertical spines of each wing.

The dragon was perched on a Babylonian cross of translucent gold that rose slowly above the surface of the crashing waves, flexing its sinewy limbs in a hateful stare, flames billowing in clouds through the sides of each fanged jowl as golden blood dripped from three slash wounds on both heads. At the same time, the dragon s rising seemed to cause the moon in the sky of his dreamworld to move to the right of the hill, revealing the image of a nighttime sun hidden behind it.

Magnus rocked back and forth on the wooden bench slowly as the dragon hovered before him in his mind, seeing his image on the mountainous hill reflected in the translucent surface of the cross. The flames of the dragon s dual jaws spiraled down around the cross, taunting him with the promise of a funeral pyre.

What do you see, Magnus? a voice whispered suddenly from the shadows.

Magnus didn t respond, unaware of a pair of silver eyes emerging from the shadows of the corner at the foot of his bench. Burnished hands slid into view from the shadows a second later, clinging to each wall of the corner just beneath the ceiling. The hem of a royal-blue robe fluttered through the air from the corner as the galley rocked back and forth on the sea, the stranger s glassy face appeared briefly in the strobes of light while the lantern swung from side to side, illuminating the intersecting walls he clung to like a spider, his thick shoulders and chest protruding forward.

What do you see, Magnus? the stranger probed encouragingly, his cosmic voice booming softly at the core of the champion s sleep-submerged consciousness.

Magnus heard the distant voice this time. I see a beast and a harlot.... And a beast with two heads, he said groggily.

And what does it all mean? the stranger asked, his eyes flashing with silver bursts of fire as his voice continued to fill the inner hull with ghostly echoes.

I.... I don t know, he answered.

That which you see is not a new revelation, the stranger answered. It is a riddle of images drawn from your knowledge of the Scriptures. Number their strength against you.... A beast, a harlot and a dragon. They shall be the triangle that tasks you in both form and legend.

Solitary tears trickled from the corners of the champion s eyes as the images in his mind started to spiral together with those of his shattered life. I.... I don t understand.

You will, the stranger replied, kindly. ....In time you will understand it all.

The stranger s silver eyes melted back into the shadows of the corner, his glassy hands sliding along the hull s wooden beams as he slowly disappeared. I am Scriptos, he echoed softly, a servant of the Lord Jesus, the risen Christ.... And I will write your story.

He was pursued on high to
suffer much for his Courage.
To inherit a Mantle prepared
for him before the foundations
of the world were laid.

The Legacy of his course has
aged well against the Wayfarer
Call, but the darkness of the
Dragon Lord grows. The wars
weigh heavy upon him.

The Shekinah Chronicles
Chronicle entry: Lisbon, 1755 A.D.

Book II

ORIGINS II: RESURRECTION

Ceaseless waves splashed against the time-worn shore of Magnus mind, thundering with memory that froze his thoughts in the past for a moment. The jagged bluffs and smooth, gray slopes of the Isle of Patmos, a small island formed by a volcanic eruption in the Aegean Sea, rose into view in his mind while he sat silently on a flat rock in a moonlit grove of cedars. The small isle had been his home for a hundred years after his initial banishment to its shores.

Magnus sank into the memory of his last day on the small island. Rome still ruled the world at the time. But Titus and Vespasian had long since died. Emperors had come and gone, but he had survived them all without aging a single day in appearance or strength.

He saw himself that last day standing on the islands ash-covered beach at sunset, the volcanic cliffs and hills looming behind as he faced the sea, the tide slapping gently against the legs of his deer skin pants, the salty breeze blowing through his collar-length hair and the thick beard covering the lower half of his sleek face. He was twirling a wooden staff in front of him that was hollowed out at each end, with several holes carved into the exterior of the staff's two ends. Ballots of air whistled through the holes in the staff as he spun it back and forth in front of him, whipping it around his back in circles while passing it from hand to hand with a virtuosos grace, filling the salty air with a sharp melody.

Magnus stopped when a flash of light and wind swept across his face. He crouched defensively with his staff, snapping his head to the right. An enormous figure of a man stood on the beach only a few feet away, appearing out of thin air, clothed in a luminous robe of sky-blue flax that had the outline of heavy armaments beneath it.

Keep those senses sharp, you beloved son of *The Way*, the hooded figure replied, his voice echoing softly with a familiar dialect. Your greatest threat will always come when you least expect it.

Magnus nodded his head while maintaining his defensive stance.

I am Gabriel, a servant of the Lord Jesus, the risen Christ, the tall visitor said, pulling back the hood of his robe to reveal a burnished face framed by disheveled locks of platinum hair, eyes bright with colors of blue, white and gold.

Magnus lowered his staff, driving it into the sand beside him, the Holy Spirit assuring him the angelic visitor was telling the truth.

The time has come for you to leave this place, Gabriel told him.

The angel reached inside his robe and pulled out a copper scroll and an old soft leather case with the mark of a *flagrum taxillatum* whip master branded on its flap. Take this scroll, he urged, offering the rolled copper first.

Magnus reached out and took the scroll from the angel s hand. What is it? he asked, taking note of the Hebrew symbols hammered into the rolled copper.

It is a map to the riches that were buried with King David beneath Jerusalem, said Gabriel. You will need it to replace the wealth of your mother s house that was stolen from you. There is a special vest of armor and a helmet hidden among the treasures as well. Be sure to take them with you.... For they are the symbols of your authority.

Magnus shook his head, remembering the legends he d been told as a child about the secret treasure Solomon had supposedly buried with his father King David. I am not worthy of such riches, he replied.

You are a prince in the House of Sheshbazzar, Magnus. They are yours by right of inheritance. But take only what you need. A mere portion of such treasure will make you the wealthiest man on the face of this Earth.... For you shall be a nomadic king of great travels to foreshadow the wrath to be poured out at the return of the King of Kings.

Magnus fell silent, glancing out at the ocean as its tide sliced softly around his feet. He could only imagine what waited for him beyond the horizon.

Gabriel offered the leather case next. And take this, he told him. But do not open it until you are instructed to do so. Keep it somewhere safe until the appointed time.

Magnus took the case by its strap and held it in front of him. Dare I ask what this is?

You will know at the appointed time.

Magnus didn t argue. He simply nodded his head and secured it across his chest by the strap it dangled from.

After you have secured the treasure of your inheritance, Gabriel continued, seek out the tomb and the iron sarcophagus of King Og of Bashan. You will need the mystery of the ancient sword in Og s tomb to help you shape your own offensive weapons of war as Michael instructed. But make sure you are not followed to the tomb. This particular sword must not fall into the wrong hands after you reseal it in the sarcophagus.

Why? he asked.

You will know the reason why once you have held it in your own hands.

With that said, Gabriel pulled the hood of his robe back over his head and began to walk away. Farewell, you beloved son of *The Way*, he said, his voice echoing across the beach. The Lord is with you always, even unto the end of the age.

Wait, Magnus pleaded, reaching out for the angel just as he had done with Michael so long ago, countless questions still plaguing him about the life set before him.

Gabriel shot into the air in a bright streak of light before even one of those remaining questions could be posed, arcing across the twilight sky above.

The sounds of the night echoed softly in Magnus hearing, slowly drawing him from the ancient memories of his last day on the Isle of Patmos.

He stirred sluggishly, massaging his eyes as the image of the angel faded from his mind. The rock where he was sitting was positioned on the ridge of a small wooded hill in southern Lebanon overlooking an enormous crater in the center of a grove of trees below. His hair was short and slickly parted to the side, eyes bright with a millennial glow. He wore a full length frock coat of brown velvet, accented by a dark-blue sweater and jeans to help ward off the cold air that swept down from the fossil-lined mountains of limestone looming all around him in the distance. Tall cedars with thick, sweeping branches towered over both sides of him like the mythic spires of a gothic castle, their dark green tops brushing against the night s twinkling canvas. The moon was unusually bright, casting sporadic shafts of lunar light down throughout the rolling grove of cedars below.

The grove was one of the last of Lebanon s famous conifers, located near the small valley town of Bshirre. A larger remnant of these once proud giants had survived millenniums of war, plunder and exporting, only to be almost totally annihilated while being used as fuel for the Beirut-Damascus Railway from 1914 to 1919.

Magnus leaned forward stoically, focusing on the center of the crater s stony floor where one of the shafts of moonlight fell. It looked as though it had been filled by hand with a dark patch of soil that didn t match the dirt of the cedar-lined ridges around the top of the crater. But the most curious element of the different-colored soil was the enormous six pointed star of Rosicrucian symbolism constructed from smaller five-pointed stars symmetrically drawn in the center of it, surrounded by a wreath-like depiction of thirteen Babylonian eagles clutching olive branches and arrows of belomancy in their talons. The five-pointed stars making up the larger star were *blazing sbas* of demonic power he knew well, the origins of their first recorded appearances in the Ancient World tracing back to the pyramids of Egypt and the Dog Star of Anubis, with links to the star of Remphan mentioned in the Book of Acts. It was also an image visible on the flags and currencies of the world s most powerful nations.

Even stranger was the phrase *Akeldama* written in front of all six points of the main star, an Aramaic passage from the Scriptures meaning place or farm of blood. He knew the phrase as well as he knew the origins of the star. What he didn t know was that the dark-colored soil had been taken from the real *Farm of Blood* located outside the ancient walls of Jerusalem, a plot of land purchased by Judas with money stolen from the Apostolic treasury. This was the very same place where Judas would eventually hang himself, yet differing in location from the potter s field purchased by the Sanhedrin with the thirty pieces of silver forsaken by the Lord s chosen betrayer.

Magnus scanned the shadows of the tree-lined border on the opposite side of the crater. There was no movement in the towering crop of trees. He imagined this would change as the evening progressed, having been drawn there from Iraq by the Holy Spirit.

Like the Massorah Magna in the margins of Holy Writ, Magnus had seen much from the peripheral corners of history s last two millenniums. But bearing witness to the conflict that was clearing the way for Babylon s resurrection was something he d been anticipating for centuries. Napoleon had schemed to resurrect her, but was denied, as were others. It was a dream of all secret societies linked together by the evil legacy of that land. But it wasn t until now, with the direction of the Harness Magi s front company the Omega Group and the bank-rich families and fraternities of the Illuminati and their Masonic Order, that such dreams were finally being realized.

With the exception of others connected to his world of uncommon existence, Magnus had seen and learned more than anyone could dream possible. Time and again he worked behind the scenes, exacting judgment, empowering the weak against cruel men with global ambitions.

But at times an old loneliness would set in, prompting the desire to know the loving touch of his wife again. Such longings for companionship were only made worse when a brother or sister in Christ passed on to glory, leaving him behind to continue his sojourn through the world. The pressures of the *Wayfarer Call* and the potency of his

Adamic nature were by far the most difficult of his wars. But the double-edged sword that had become his life often sang with a bittersweet promise of release, especially when it openly clashed with the razor-sharp edges of mankind s wickedness.

Such were the wars he greeted with both dread and welcome.

———•>•‹•———

Magnus sat for long, uninterrupted hours on the rock as the midnight hour approached.

He glanced up through the treetops of the cedars surrounding his elevated perch as a frigid wind swept across his stony face. A distant beacon of multicolored light caught his attention as it fell slowly from the stars in the Outer Realm. It appeared to be a meteorite at first, but the anomaly grew brighter as it fell. He lost sight of it behind the mountains before he could magnify it with his preternatural vision.

He figured it to be a host of some kind. The heavens over the Middle East had been filled with a greater intensity of angelic activity ever since the beginning of the war to raise Babylon from the ashes, especially when the Imperial Fortress of the enemy arrived over the city of Al-Hilla.

He leaned forward, training his gaze on the trees opposite the crater, hoping to discover the reason he had been led to this dark hole in the world.

He soon did.

Careful, Magnus, a voice echoed softly from behind. The darkness can master you with too much study.... Especially on this Christmas Eve night.

Magnus sat up slowly at the sound of the frigid voice, eyes darting back and forth. He didn t turn as a pair of white, slanted eyes appeared behind him in the shadows, followed by the bronze silhouette of sharply-tipped wings. The assassin s burning eyes hovered about ten feet high in the air, his wingspan filling the space between two trees behind the rock, covering his mountainous shoulders like a rippling suit of liquid armor.

He kept his gaze straight ahead, confused by the fact his sensitive hearing and acutely tuned perception of the angelic realm had failed in warning him of the rebel s approach. But the overwhelming veil of dread filling the atmosphere around him clearly told him what sort of host he was dealing with.

Magnus didn t move, ready to defend himself in the blink of an eye as he decided to question the rebel to gauge any other hidden strengths he possessed. How is it that you know my name, fallen one? he asked, glancing back out of the corner of his left eye.

A fanged smile appeared in the shadow beneath the flesh-peeling heat of the assassin s white eyes. It s my business to know, he answered.

Really?... You must be Old Scratch himself, then?

A muffled chuckle shrouded Magnus from behind, the assassin s eyes pulsing malevolently. No.... But you can think of me as the *Devil s Fiddler*, if you like.

Magnus gave little heed to the assassin s boastful comment, keeping his mind trained as sharply as possible on the position of the entity s voice. Let me warn you, rebel. I have little patience for games tonight.

The assassin hissed with a soft laughter. Such arrogance.... I like that in a man.

Magnus swivelled sideways, catching a glimpse of the sharp edges of the assassin s metallic wingspan outlined by a shaft of moonlight. Your blood-soaked plunder of this world will not last forever. Judgment is promised. And it will be a swift and unforgiving hand that deals it.

The assassin smiled widely again when he saw something approaching the crater s opposite ridge. Promises are meant to be broken, he said, pointing, revealing a thick arm that glistened like black marble in the moonlight. Behold those who would welcome the Dragon Lord s age of uncontested rule....

Magnus was slow to turn, keeping his mind tuned to the assassin s position. His eyes fell on the crater once more. An unusually tall and brutish man dressed in a black overcoat and suit walked to the crater s edge, stopping in a shaft of moonlight that fell between two trees along its rounded border. He wore a small skull and crossbones pin on the left lapel of his coat. His hair was short and black, fashionably slicked to the side, his face dark and olive-colored. The portals of his eye sockets appeared empty beneath the depth of shadows veiling them.

Magnus immediately recognized the giant. He hadn t crossed paths with the Nephilimite known as Tsavo since the night of his coronation. But he had encountered many of the vampire demoni-acs and secret societies allied to Tsavo since then, with one of the more notable of such skirmishes taking place on the out-skirts of London during the Great Plague of the 17th century as he sought to recap-ture a dark and ancient sword from his past.

A downward rush of wind fell sud-denly through the surrounding trees as another power entered the wooded arena.

A scarlet, black-winged prince fell to the center of the crater from the night s brightly lit canopy, his taloned feet stirring up a clap of thunder with his touchdown next to the six pointed star. The rebel was arrayed in a jeweled, black-muscled cuirass, flashes of yellow fire rotating in the center of each shadowy eye, fangs glowing in the shafts of moonlight blanketing the spot where he stood. He relaxed his wings, turning his back to Magnus lofty perch on the tree-lined hill to face the giant standing above him on the crater s opposite ridge, motioning him forward.

Magnus watched intently as Tsavo leaped to the stony floor of the crater, landing on the other side of the star across from the familiar rebel. The Nephilimite stood eye level with Sodom, saluting him with a quick bow of his dark head. No words were exchanged as they both stepped back from the star several paces. Their attention was drawn toward the star at their feet, as if waiting for something to happen.

Magnus didn t move, trying to keep his focus on the rebel still lingering behind him.

The assassin moved closer to the shaft of light where he had unveiled his arm, allowing his towering form to become more defined. Behold, champion, he said, holding out his large left hand to reveal the ashes of an ancient corpse. Behold ... the rise of Perdition s Son.

Magnus stiffened from a wind stirred up around him, spoken into existence by the rebel s voice. The wind scattered the pile of ashes in the assassin s hand, gathering them together in a cluster of shadows that swept toward the center of the crater. Tsavo and Sodom stepped back from the star again as the wind encompassed them, the shadows swirling in and around them, howling fiercely as they pierced the shafts of moonlight, mixing with the eagle and star-shaped symbols of the darkly-colored soil at the center of the crater floor.

The ash and dirt-filled shadows circled the crater s center as a flash of divine lightning struck the middle of the crater like an atomic key. The ground opened with a thunderous cracking from the force of the strike that continued down through the Earth, creating a fissure that stretched deep beneath the floor of the Mediterranean Sea miles away. The rim of the hole turned counterclockwise as the fissure formed beneath it, its stones churning like water.

Black smoke bellowed from the hole as the sides of the newly formed pit quickly hardened to a six-foot diameter, releasing a funnel of wind that rocked the tops of the surrounding trees, rippling the night s starry stream with a fervent heat.

Tsavo and Sodom stood their ground outside the host of shadows circling the opening in the crater floor, listening to Teraphimic wails exploding from the mouth of the pit like the roar of a thousand cannons.

The opaque arm of a human spirit emerged slowly through the smoke, beckoned from a place of wandering imprisonment in the *well* of the Abyss, fingers wide and probing as they clamped down on the stony sides of the pit. Another arm followed, its hand gripping the stones in like manner, with the head and shoulders of the *nephesh*-crowned spirit emerging next.

The pit closed in a clockwise motion behind the man-shaped spirit after he climbed free, severing the smoke and tormented winds of his prison.

Sodom and the giant stared at the resurrected spirit wailing at their feet.

Above the crater, Magnus stood, horrified. It can t be, he whispered.

The assassin laughed. But it is, he assured him. Behold.... *The Beast that was, and is not, and yet is*!

The assassin s words echoed down the slope with his quote from the Book of the Revelation, stirring the circling ashes around the spirit as he rolled over on his back in the center of the crater, mummifying him in the orbiting vapors of new life. The ashes from the ancient corpse and the dirt from the *Farm of Blood* began forming a skeleton over the spirit s shady form, knitting the joints together like simple building blocks, rib cage snapping together in a flash of light. A new brain covered the spirit s opaque mind, its rippled substance literally drawn into existence by one of the smoky fingers of the orbiting ash. A smooth skull appeared afterwards, formed in the same manner. Cerebral tendrils extended from beneath the skull, attaching to the spinal cord as the rest of the needed organs and blood vessels emerged from the molecules of the ancient corpse s ashy remains, giving rise to muscles and other tissue that bloated and stretched in and around the skeleton, completing its intricate network. Eyes swelled into view beneath closed lids while the exterior flesh of the spirit s new body was being created, followed by long tresses of black hair mixed with translucent highlights of gold that sprouted from his scalp. The ashy vapors swirled around his face, leaving behind a smooth layer of flawless bronze skin as the dirt and ash-filled shadows dissolved at the bottom of his feet.

The resurrected man lay motionless in the center of the crater as the howling winds died away, entombed in his new flesh, awaiting the final fusion between body, soul and spirit.

Sodom stepped forward, reaching to the belt of his armored apron and pulling out a golden drinking horn of metaphysical design. It was an ornate cup shaped like a winged lion, with the rear half of its body extending up through its wings in the shape of a gilded horn with a wide mouth and diabolical markings of archaic skill.

Sodom knelt beside the head of the resurrected man, pulling back the lid of the drinking horn with his sharp fingers as he lowered it towards the open mouth of the body s flawless face that was identical to one he had worshiped for ages. Receive all that the great Seraph offers, Lord Judas.... *For out of the serpent s root shall come forth a cockatrice, and his fruit shall be a fiery flying serpent,* he said, quoting a passage from the Book of Isaiah.

The liquid was a black, blood-like crude alchemized from the jeweled substance of the Dragon Lord s own body. It rushed down Judas throat like a pathogenic flame, filling his new organs and blood vessels with its thunderous charge, hardening his entire body inside and out to a preternatural state, merging his soul-crowned spirit with the carbon-based brain of his new body in a completing jolt of power.

Sodom stood after pouring the last of the blood into Judas mouth, securing the drinking horn on his belt again.

Stars filled the spectrum of Judas blue eyes as his eyelids flew open suddenly, mouth gaping open even further with the first rush of air into his ageless lungs. The memories of his last night on Earth flooded his newly formed brain. His breaths became shorter and faster at the passing image of a familiar Carpenter who stood bound in the Garden of Gethsemane. The memory of a crooked tree quickly followed. A thick, twisting rope was clenched in the left hand of his former body as he saw himself standing beneath the tree. The image of the Tyrian shekels paid to him by the Sanhedrin had been his last thoughts in the land of the living, their silver luster shattered by a quick snap of twine. The memory of the sudden snap caused him to scream when a blistering abode darkened the vision in his mind.

His screams stopped abruptly as the vision of darkness in his mind quickly gave way to his earthly surroundings, his thoughts drawn to the cool breeze brushing over his sleek-muscled frame, arousing his senses with prickly prods of new life. The reality of his long-desired freedom was almost unbelievable at first, after wandering through the dry places of torment in the *well* of the Abyss for the last two millenniums.

He lifted his hands to his face as the sweet sensation of freedom swept over him, the dust-size particles of his old body falling from his fingers, dissolving with a familiar scent of judgment that had cankered his spirit for centuries, hardening him to the core with a purpose as dark as the prison that had held him for so long. This was a purpose he could never have understood before his fall. But Jesus had known. He had even declared it boldly before all the Apostles. The memory of that day had tortured him with the same viciousness as the darkened flames of the Abyss. But his memories of the Old Testament Scriptures spoke to him in his torment like never before when he was alive, revealing to him a future time when he would be allowed a season of opportunity to challenge God for control of the universe and its focus of worship. It was an opportunity he had anticipated with great scheme.

Judas pulled his knees toward him, rising from the center of the crater slowly without using his hands or bending at the waist, quickened by the immense power of the Dragon Lord s blood flowing through his darkened mind. He stood six feet tall, the tresses of his ethereal hair twisting slightly in a gust of wind.

Pin needles of light exploded across his blue eyes the moment he sensed Sodom s presence. The armored rebel stood before him in all his dark glory, his false wings swaying in the soft currents of the night air.

Judas strutted toward the rebel angel, raising his arms as if to embrace him. He looked up into Sodom s black eyes, gazing at the mirror-like irises of yellow fire reflecting his new veneer, the dual images contorting like the flickers of a candle light. A god and not a man, he said, focusing on the rebel s face with a vain smile, his voice devoid of accent as it echoed softly in a rapid-fire succession of every language spoken among humans, angels and the Cherubim. I was speaking of myself, of course.

Sodom bowed. Of course, he agreed. Such godhood warrants my devotion to you, Lord Judas.... That is why we have been sent to you. To prepare you for your anointed place as the Great Tree who will rule over the nations.

Judas looked at the giant standing silently to his right, receiving a reluctant nod from him. He could sense the giant s immediate jealousy of him, and he liked it. The mere size and regal bearing of the giant, coupled with the Dragon Lord s supernatural knowledge of Tsavo flowing through him, told him that he was one of the old ones; a Nephilimite like the conquerors of renown from the Antediluvian World. With obvious jealousies and added knowledge aside, such a lineage alone made the giant one to be watched carefully.

The master has also sent you a gift, said Sodom, turning to the trees behind him.

Judas and Tsavo both faced the border of trees as Sodom gave a guttural command to the shadow-filled spaces between the cedars above the crater s rim. A man dressed in a silver robe with a large hood stepped through the tall cedars, followed by twelve demon possessed men arrayed in hooded, black capes draped over panoply mixtures of Assyrian, Babylonian and Persian body armor.

Tsavo growled softly when the leader of the small band of men appeared, glancing back at Sodom suspiciously.

The man in the silver robe walked down into the crater, carrying a large, ancient chest in front of him. The others behind him followed his lead to the crater floor.

The leader stopped when he reached the bottom of the slope, waiting for his men to march ahead and form their lines of tribute. The men turned and faced one another in two lines, making a quick draw of their sickle swords before dropping to one knee in a unified clatter of armor, extending their shimmering blades across the crater s floor.

The leader made his way slowly through the aisle, keeping his eyes on the curved lid of the chest he was carrying. The chest was crafted from lacquered acacia wood and fitted with ornamental emblems and hinges of pure gold. No key hole was visible on the front of the lid, but rather a large thick seal of silver. A carving of a lion s head protruded from the seal, its fanged mouth open as if to strike, eyes large and hollow.

The leader stopped at the end of the aisle, dropping to one knee with the others, placing the chest on the crater floor.

He glanced at the rebel angel towering to his right, seeing the same terrible appearance he had observed many times before during the dark rituals of his secret order, designed to prepare him for this very moment. The men behind him were each Adeptus Exemptus magicians versed in a perversely titled system of *magick* known as the Enochian Key; a subordinate sorcery of invocations giving them the power to steel themselves when looking upon rebel masters. It was a power acquired through intense training that included memorizing the Satanic Grimoires; ancient books of sorcery like the infamous Necronomicon.

Bestow the gift, Sodom ordered.

The leader pulled back his hood, revealing a mark on the back of his right hand. The mark was shaped like a black griffin cresting over the top of a golden cross, constricted by a black and red dragon with two heads. The leader s silver hair and tanned face had the appearance of a countenance halted at middle-age, preserved in that state by an ancient power flowing from a staff known as the *Oracle of the Dragon Lord* strapped across his back in a long quiver.

Judas recognized him from images in the Dragon Lord s blood flowing through his brain.

The leader focused on the chest in front of him. He reached into his robe and pulled out a small pouch made of leather, fishing out two large diamonds from inside, inserting them into the hollow eyes of the lion s head emblem protruding from the chest s silver seal. Small flashes of light pulsated through the diamonds when he inserted them into the eye sockets, with air spewing from beneath the seal s thick border.

Tsavo watched with an almost salivating interest while the chest was being opened.

The leader pushed the rounded lid back slowly, reaching inside with both hands. He stood up, pulling a blackened lion-skin garment from the chest, tailored by Satan himself from a rare breed of lion descending from the Genesis lineage of its species that had been spared destruction in the Second Great Deluge.

The *Covenant Harness* hung like a cloak in the leader s hands as he made sure not to touch the black, scale-like lining of the skin s interior. It was designed in six, wing-like segments, with silver-tipped bear claws looped to the tapered hem of the front and back wings. Red, eagle-style feathers were sewn to each segment of the harness by vertical threads of adamantine, with nine types of eye-shaped jewels embedded like scales throughout the feathered segments in a vast display of wealth. Silver, crescent moons arced over each jewel to complete its armored look.

Dual leopard heads were fastened to both of the garment s shoulders, with their lower jaws having been removed in the design process. Each beast once weighed two hundred pounds more than their modern day descendants now ranging from the plains of the Serengeti to the rim of Mount Kilimanjaro s Kibo Crater.

A blackened cowl constructed from the head of the lion skin harness itself hung forward from the back segments of the garment, its lower mouth having been removed like the garment s beastly shoulder crowns, with its original eyes replaced by the golden orbs of a dragon. The cowl s upper mouth dangled from an iron chain with a Quicksilver enamel, connecting the space between the garment s front segments, anchored to sun-shaped emblems of embossed gold depicting black and red dragons intertwined in poses of broken infinity. Gold engraving plates were molded in the centers of the chain s thick links, displaying bronze-colored titles of authority such as *The Assyrian, Prince of Tyre, King of Babylon* and *The Son of Perdition*; each written with a stylus-tooled precision in various Semitic languages. Another emblem of gold depicting a black and red shepherd wrapped in the mantle skins of a wolf hung down from the chain s central link, with a long, silver-coated spike that was squared in its design hooked to the bottom. The words, *The*

Nail, were carved in a single column of black Hebrew letters on the front of the spike; the same one once used to hold the third and final disputed epitaph above the head of the Lord Jesus, which read, *This is the King of the Jews*.

The symbols of the harness had been added to the original garment over time, with each holding great significance. The garment s beastly shoulder crowns represented the great Leopard Kingdom of the future, and not that of Alexander the Great s empire that was divided up after his death between his four generals Ptolemy, Cassander, Lysimachus and Seleucus. The bear claws dangling from the split hems of the front and back wings were also future in their symbolism. The feathers of the harness represented the eagle standard once used by the Serpent Tribe of Dan; a segment of people who disappeared from the nation of Israel as a formative group thousands of years ago when Tiglath Pileser III of Assyria invaded the land and took a great number of Danites into captivity. The lion s-head cowl was a symbol of a future power as well. But the garment as a whole was meant to represent the entire global kingdom to be embodied in the person of the Great Tree. This messiah would reign over the world through ten kings from joint commands in Babylon, Tyre and Pergamos, all overseen by the fatherly eyes of the dragon.

Tsavo stepped to the side of Judas several paces to get a better look at the garment. Though he had never seen it before, he knew he was looking upon the garment of his ancient lust for the first time.

Judas blue eyes danced with delight as he, too, recognized the garment. Its legend in the Ancient World had no equal. Its wearer would inherit the covenant power of the Archrebel himself, a covenant revealed to him during his torturous wandering throughout the Abyss.

The leader showed no concern for the giant s sudden edginess upon laying his hardened eyes on the ancient treasure for the first time. Though Tsavo was a formidable force to be reckoned with, he had been easily denied from obtaining the harness for millenniums by each of the Magi Masters. Tonight would be no different.

The leader formally offered the armor of promise to the future king. To you, Lord Judas, I present the *Covenant Harness*.

Tsavo growled with a low, guttural hate at the leader s words. His desire for the *Covenant Harness* was insatiable. He d always known it would be unveiled one day. But he had expected its appearance to come just prior to Judas ascension to a global throne. Not now. Not at a moment when he was unprepared to take action.

Sodom gave Tsavo a fiery stare, flashing his large, wickedly-sharp fangs in silent laughter. He turned fully toward the giant, resting his black-nailed hand on the hilt of his blade in a threatening gesture.

Tsavo s fists clenched at his sides as the leader passed in front of him. He glanced at Sodom in his threatening pose, quickly peering back at the garment so very near to him, his heart thundering with primordial instinct.

Scores of Sodom s best warriors began to surround the crater s ridges, their red and yellow eyes appearing in the shadows like scattering embers.

The giant took his eyes off the garment, growling under his breath at the sudden arrival of the Nekros Order. There would be no escape should he act to seize the harness now. He could only stand by and watch while it was presented to Judas, his strength having been contained by superior numbers.

Judas tilted his head back as the leader lifted the garment s chain above him. He spread his arms outward to let the vestment s black-scaled lining slide down over his arms and back, gasping with a sudden delight when the fabled harness came to a rest on his shoulders with a velveteen weight, its pendant and spike sliding down to the center of his chest, the garment s tapered hems with the dangling bear claws swishing down around his knees.

The leader walked in front of Judas, waiting silently.

Judas looked ahead regally as he reached behind to pull the sides of the beastly cowl forward. The two ivory fangs of the cowl s upper mouth sank down on each side of his eyes as the crown came to a rest on his head, revealing the word *Alchemy* inscribed in golden letters on the forehead of the lion just beneath its arcing mane of black hair; written in several Semitic languages. In similar manner, the phrase, *The Lie*, was carved in red on each fang of the cowl.

The sides of the lion s hollowed-out neck surrounded his throat the moment he lowered his hands, the harness crown amplifying the power within him in a sudden jolt of energy. The whole garment gave him the appearance of a fierce cherub.

The leader motioned to his men behind him to stand up as Judas relished the crown s amplifying power. I, Simon Menelaus, Master of the Harness Magi and keeper of the *Oracle of the Dragon Lord*, bid you welcome, Lord Judas, he replied. And we bring you tidings of Babylon s rise.... All phases of Operation Assyria and Project Palladium are proceeding according to the master s plan.

I know, said Judas. And I am well pleased.

We of the Magi, as our deceased brethren of the Cainites of long ago, have clung to the prophecy of the ascended masters that you would rise again one day. We believed you would stand up against the Lion of the Tribe of Judah himself as in the past. For that, we are your servants. And we have come to worship you.

Simon bowed his head and knee with a worshipful decree. O king, live forever.

The other Magi behind Simon prostrated themselves in the same manner, raising their swords as they repeated the sorcerer s words. O king, live forever!!

Sodom bowed and repeated the chorus of praise himself. O king, live forever!

Yes! Judas replied rapturously. Honor me!

Sodom lifted his head from where he knelt, peering over at the giant who refused to relinquish his proud stance.

Judas turned towards the giant at the same time, hardening his pose against the defiant Nephilimite as he spoke to him for the first time. I am your king now, Tsavo, he commanded. I must increase. But you must decrease.... Honor me.

Tsavo glared down at the Beast with a restrained hate. His movement was slow in the bowing of his knee and head. Hail to you, Lord Judas, he said lowly, fists clenched tightly by his sides, black blood seeping through his fingers from the bite of his razor-sharp fingernails.

Judas laughed with delight, turning toward the others kneeling before him. I accept your honor, he replied, glancing at the fiery eyes that lingered in the shadows around the moonlit crater. But hear me. Though the gravity of the Abyss still chains me from ascending higher, I am no longer the man the world briefly knew. No longer the zealot in a drama that branded me a traitor. No! Judas is dead. I am the new shepherd. The world will yield to the crook of my staff. They will follow me, Iscarius Alchemy.... And they shall worship me as their god!

The rebel angels in the surrounding trees erupted in a unified roar of praise. HAIL THE ALCHEMY KING!!! HAIL THE ALCHEMY KING!!!

———

Magnus stood galvanized by the unholy nativity unfolding in the crater below. The Unclean Spirit, he said in a haunted voice, recalling passages from the books of Zechariah and Matthew. The Antichrist.

Yesss, the assassin hissed behind him. The Fisher King has come. The Phoenix of Phoenicia. The Superman of the Serpent Tribe of Dan.... The Cockatrice of the Chaldeans.

Magnus spun around to face the rebel behind him for the first time.

The assassin pulled his wings back into the shadows, allowing only his white eyes and diamond fangs to be visible.

Who are you? Magnus demanded, squinting to try and penetrate the darkened veil covering the rebel s face.

Laughter echoed throughout the forest as the assassin sank even farther into the shadows.

Magnus stood paralyzed by an old boyhood fear as a familiar and frigid gust of wind swept across his confused face, watching the mysterious entity melt completely into the shadows as if he were one with them.

Magnus whipped back around, unsure of what to do.

Alchemy turned toward him suddenly, sensing his presence for the first time above the cheers of the rebel angels. The Master s betrayer locked gazes with him the moment he spied his tree-covered position on the slope high above the crater.

The image of the Beast enlarged when Magnus focused his stare, zooming in on his flawless face beneath the lion s-head cowl. He looked puzzled as the Beast smiled at him, choosing not to alert those worshiping him at the center of the crater. It was clear from his devilish smile that

Judas somehow recognized him from the dark power flowing through his mind.

Magnus remembered the dream he d had of the Beast while imprisoned in the belly of that Roman slave galley.

He turned his back to the Beast, searching the darkness again for a glimpse of the mysterious rebel, wondering who he really was.

Magnus was slow to face the crater again. The Beast just smiled at him as silently as before, still choosing not to alert his presence to Sodom and the others. The whole scene was even stranger than the ancient dream given to him in the bowels of that Roman slave galley. It was a nightmare beyond all his expectations.

The words of the Holy Spirit came softly and unexpectedly as Magnus stared at Judas. *Behold the Assyrian was a cedar in Lebanon with fair branches, and with a shadowing shroud, and of an high stature; and his top was among the thick boughs. The waters made him great, the deep set him up on high with her rivers running round about his plants, and sent out her little rivers unto all the trees of the field, and his boughs were multiplied, and his branches became long because of the multitude of waters, when he shot forth. All the fowls of heaven made their nests in his boughs, and under his branches did all the beasts of the field bring forth their young, and under his shadow dwelt all great nations.*

Magnus almost swayed while the Spirit-breathed words of the Prophet Ezekiel echoed in his mind, intoxicating him with a divine confirmation that what he was witnessing was not a dream.

Judas nodded at Magnus as if to tip his crown, whispering the full translation of the champion s name and surname in the same soft manner as the Lord s voice that had just spoken to him.

Magnus stiffened in his posture at the Beast s apparent mimicry of the Lord s voice. He snapped the lapels of his coat together angrily, leaping into the air with a quick thought to distance himself from the flesh-born nightmare. The forest canopy was beneath his boots in a matter of seconds. He held his head low while gripping the lapels of his coat, the wind rolling along the contours of his face.

He knew no matter how far he flew he could not escape the reality of what he d just witnessed. The Beast was alive. Many pretenders to the ultimate throne of evil had preceded him throughout the centuries. But things were eternally different now. Judas had returned as the Scriptures foretold he would. The rebel fowls of the air had been setting things in motion for centuries, waiting for the day when God would allow *The Lie* to rise from the *well* of the Abyss. A day that had finally come.

Magnus closed his eyes. The factions of peace and horror were already at war within him.

The end is not yet, my son. And now you know what is restraining, that he may be revealed in his own time. For the Mystery of Iniquity is already at work; only He who now restrains will do so until He is taken out of the way, the Lord whispered through the wind, reminding him of who was in control. *And then the Wicked One will be revealed, whom the Lord will consume with the breath of His mouth and destroy with the brightness of His coming.*

Magnus sank into the starry sky with a slumbering flight, the Spirit of the Lord guiding him across the horizon like countless times in the past. The dream of ascending from the dark road he had traveled for so long was nearer than ever before.

"Woe to the worthless shepherd,
Who leaves the flock!
A sword shall be against his arm
And against his right eye;
His arm shall completely wither,
And his right eye shall be totally
Blinded."

Zechariah 11:17

Book III

ORIGINS III:
ICHABOD

Tower Valley, a small, prosperous town of twenty-two thousand located north of San Francisco near the Oregon border, was sprawled out on a slightly rolling plain drenched in spring sunlight. The town was surrounded by thick forests and a range of mountains shaped like a natural coliseum, the slopes and cliffs of the granite peaks covered with towering pines stretching down around the foothills all the way to Pacific Coast Highway 101.

Once known as Tsidkenu Valley long ago, the town had since become a picture of progressing economic achievement since its expansion from the original site on the eastern mountain range; a settlement founded in 1860 by Jewish Christians. The town was a small metropolis with the grandeur of the old and the new intertwined in its structures. The streets were paved with fresh asphalt. Traffic was moderate as the town s citizens roamed back and forth between the different shops along Main Street. South of the business district were rows of brilliantly carved balustrades, towering pillars, second floor porticos, shingled cupolas, daunting arches, emerald green lawns, and black, wrought-iron fences. These were the crown jewels of the posh Victorian homes dominating that section of town. Most of the older structures were nestled in the heart of the town s executive community known as Imperial Lane, each differing with a signature roofline.

The local courthouse stood at the northern core of the town. It was an imposing sight, modeled after the likeness of London s Westminster Abbey, with gothic spires towering into the sky on each of the rectangular structure s four corners. Hundreds of stone arches covered the frontal facade, enclosing portals of reflective glass. An enormous clock tower made of smooth, gray stone, with an obelisk-crowned roof and a horizontally ribbed exterior, reached hundreds of feet into the skyline from the middle of an open courtyard in the center of the square-shaped courthouse. Men on steel scaffolds surrounded the lower half of the tower, slowly making their way upward while overlapping the stone exterior with strips of pure ivory carved with intricately detailed images of winged, Virgoan goddesses riding upon Taurus bulls.

Four identical glass buildings surrounded the courthouse, the clock tower rising high above their flat roofs. L-shaped tunnels of plexiglass extended from the sides of the buildings, connecting each of the new structures that were surrounded by more men on steel scaffolds completing the final stages of a year-long construction plan. Like the monuments of Egypt and Washington D.C., the four glass buildings, as ordered by the Omega Group, had been aligned according to ancient astrological blueprints of the Zodiac. Even the streets intersecting with the courthouse square, designed by the town s first Masonic insurgents over a hundred years ago, mirrored the cosmic causeways of Rome and Babylon in their north-south trajectories. The transpatial archeometry of the buildings and the streets intersecting with the courthouse were designed to mark the town as a stronghold for demons and rebel angels; an esoteric *magick* found in varying forms in government buildings and churches across the globe, perpetuating the motto of the ancients: *As above, so below.*

A steady stream of armored SUVs with tinted windows roamed back and forth throughout the town, taking care of business for the Omega Group; an international conglomerate secretly established by the Harness Magi on December 24th 1913 with the billions of dollars in gold and other natural resources horded over the centuries by the predecessors of their mystic order. Crews from the Omega Group s Special Services Corps, an elite communications team responsible for installation of electronic countermeasures, were busy installing fiber optic EMP charges beneath the roads throughout the town and surrounding valley. The charges would be capable of instantly crippling vehicles of any size with an electromagnetic pulse.

Black Hawk helicopters flew back and forth from a small air base built just outside of town at the foot of the valleys northern mountain range, with a set of railroad tracks located nearby that had been limited to supply traffic only. The base was fenced off with the tightest of security, complete with barracks large enough to house a small team of elite soldiers recruited by the Omega Group. A heavily protected gatehouse was built next to the fenced off facility, guarding entry to a road leading up to a wide plain in the foothills of the northern mount where a 17th century-style French chateau could be partially seen looming above the air base, its shingled roofs cresting just above the treetops on the mountains lower slope.

Rebel angels hovered unseen high above the bustling town, formed in a ring consisting of twenty-four elite warriors from the Nekros Order. They rotated slowly around the clock towers black-numbered face that was enclosed in a leafy trim on all four sides, counseling with one another telepathically in great anticipation of the arrival of their Shadow King from the port city of San Francisco.

The rebels had infiltrated the town during its expansion of the original settlement, paving the way for one of the temples of the Masonic Order that put its roots down in the valley at the turn of the century. The Masonic newcomers to the town turned out to be not only allies and relatives of California s Railroad Barons and Silver Kings, but also wolves from an ancient order of cabalism that had veiled themselves in the folds of the Church and various charities since the days of the Apostles. The Gold Rush of 1849 first brought them to the state, increasing their wealth, and allowing them to gobble up territory for their own personal use and development. Their land grabs would eventually bring them to the valley. And with the lure of their formidable resources, they would gain influence with some of the children of the original settlers holding prominent positions in the town s government. Their lust for control spoiled forty years of peace by pushing those from power who were spiritually aware of their Luciferian doctrines cleverly masked in charity and religion. Most of those who resisted them in one form or another were murdered. These dark deeds were conveniently covered up by the

town s new, Masonically-contracted police
and judiciary branches of service brought
in from San Francisco in the year1900. The
majority of the town, however, would con-
form to the Pergamos and Laodicean spiri-
tuality that had crept in amongst them
with the purpose and drive of progress at
any cost; a compromise foreshadowing the
corrupting spirits that would assault the
seven future Jewish assemblies of Asia
Minor the Apostle John had written to in
the Revelation of Jesus Christ.

As a result of such apostasy, the town
was later marked for total darkness by an
epitaph that had mysteriously appeared
above the archway of the town s house of
worship. It manifested sometime between
Halloween and the morning eve of the
Babylonian holiday All Saints Day, exactly
six months and *thirteen* days after the
great earthquake that struck San Francisco in 1906. The word *Ichabod* had literally been cut into the sanctuary s granite
stonework; an Old Testament curse which
meant the glory of God had departed. And
it had. For there had not been a trace of
true Faith in the town for over a hundred
years.

———

Gabriel, one of the seven princes
from the Order of the Watchers, stood
unseen in the belfry of the town s clock
tower, awash in a mix of shadows and rays

of sunlight pouring through the belfry s stone arches. Crisscrossing beams of wood filled the belfry s vaulted ceiling above him, with long-stemmed pistons and steel spindles hanging down between them, supporting three large brass bells hovering above a square opening in the wooden floor beneath them.

Heavy armaments were outlined beneath the luminous robe of sky-blue flax he was wearing, his platinum hair accentuating the glow of his burnished, man-shaped face. Swirls of light emanated from his gold pupils and white irises, pulsing back and forth across the surfaces of his solid-blue corneas, filtering outward from the sides of his eyes in vaporous streams while he watched the rebel angels circle the tower. His presence in the bell tower went undetected by the rebels thanks to an angelic and cherubic diffraction veil the Order of the Watchers and the Book Masters of Heaven were gifted with. But it was only a temporary veil.

Gabriel turned his head to the right suddenly as he sensed a familiar presence. His peripheral vision allowed him to see a dark-haired figure of a man sifting through the belfry s middle bell in fiery ripples, the train of his long, royal-blue coat of modern design swirling down around his legs in the draft of his sudden appearance.

Did you get the deed? Gabriel asked.

The angel bowed his head. It is done, my prince, he said. The old sanctuary on the valley s eastern mountain range has been secured for the champion. All records of its existence have been destroyed as you ordered.

Were you detected?

No, my prince.

Well done, Scriptos.... Well done.

Scriptos stepped to Gabriel s side in front of the open arch where the Nekros warriors could be seen circling the tower, the menace of their red and yellow eyes rolling in through the belfry like the embers of a suffocating furnace.

This town s curse is a heavy one, Scriptos commented, silver light streaming from the sides of his eyes as he watched the rebels circle the tower.

Yes, Gabriel agreed. The task will be grim, especially with the imminent arrival of Sodom the Sullier.

I understand there is activity in the Outer Realm because of the activity here?

Gabriel nodded. The evil one s Dominium Gate Masters are fortifying their positions. But that s not unusual at this late hour. They ve been fortifying their blockades since the allies of Apostate Israel started clearing the way for the king-doms of the Great Tree.

Gabriel gave the angel a stare of warning. But the evil one and his Alchemy King are not satisfied with their advances, he added, slowly turning his attention back to the rotating ring of rebels. That s why they ve invested so heavily in this valley project.

Scriptos turned to the arch again. I dare say the champion will feel the full force of the evil one s triangle here.

To be sure. For this town s cup of wickedness is almost full.

Both focused silently on the *Ichabod* epitaph cut into the stonework of the town s sanctuary that was being torn down a few blocks away from their position. They had both witnessed the consequences of such wickedness many times throughout history. And the result was always the same. Wrath and judgment.

Such a curse is not so easily removed, Scriptos remarked, watching a large crane and wrecking ball go to work on the sanctuary s small bell tower.

No.... It never is.

Gabriel lifted his line of sight again. The Nekros warriors were starting to rap violently on their shields with their sickle swords, howling with goblin shrills in celebration of the collapse of the sanctuary s frontal facade where the *Ichabod* epitaph had been carved.

Gabriel turned away from the arch and started toward the bells. Come, he said. Our season in this hell is finished for now.

They strode across the belfry floor with ghostly steps, rippling through the middle brass bell like pools of fiery water, dropping down through the square opening in the floor beneath the bells, disappearing into the darkness of the tower s four-hundred-dred-foot well.

Depart from Me, you cursed, into the everlasting fire prepared for the Devil and his angels.

Matthew 25:41

Book IV

CHAPTER 1

A cheviot-red Aston Martin DB7 screamed around the winding curves in the forests of Tower Valley s southern foothills, its halogen headlights slicing sharply through the night. The milky-skinned driver glanced into the rear view mirror, her hazel eyes squinting from the glare of the pursuing headlights reflected in the glass. The perfect features of her face were tense and desperate as she brushed away the auburn locks from her face, tossing them over the shoulder of her blue Chanel suit. She scanned the road ahead, jamming on the clutch, shifting through the gears frantically. A surge of adrenaline pumped through her toned legs while working the pedals repeatedly, the steering wheel trembling softly in her hand with each stomp on the gas.

April Wedding, a gifted scientist and mother of a six-year-old daughter, was running from a future threatening to steal all traces of her identity, and ultimately damn her soul.

Hang on, baby, April replied, glancing at her daughter buckled in the passenger seat beside her, bracing her hand against the child s chest as she whipped the Aston Martin around another sharp curve, tires squealing as the tachometer reached 90 mph.

Stop, momma! Please! the child begged, crushing a fluffy toy lamb against the breast of her denim overalls.

Everything s gonna be okay, Megan, she said, glancing back at the relentless headlights in the rear view mirror. We just have to get away from here as quickly as we can.

The black Suburban behind her rocked back and forth, struggling to keep pace through the tight curves in the road, headlights fixed on high beam to blind her.

The chase continued for several minutes through the treacherous turns until a long stretch of road with steep banks on each side opened up before the speeding vehicles. The Suburban was able to close some of the distance between it and the Aston Martin, narrowing the margin to about five car lengths.

April reached up and slapped the rear view mirror downward in a fit of rage, severing the blinding lights it reflected. She pressed her petite-heeled foot on the gas even harder, the car s speed dangerously passing 100 mph.

Megan looked at her mother with frightful tears. Momma, stop! We re going too fast!

April dared not take her eyes off the road at such speeds to attempt to console her daughter, painfully ignoring her pleas to slow down.

Momma, please!

April stared straight ahead into the darkness. Megan, momma needs you to be quiet right now, she said desperately.

No!... I m scared.

Megan, please!

Something in the distance caught April s attention while she argued with her daughter. Another set of headlights exploded into view a quarter of a mile away from a second SUV. It slid sideways to block the road, causing her to let up on the gas instantly to slow the speeding car.

April started to panic as she was suddenly faced with the prospect of being captured. She tried to muddle through her jumbled thoughts of what to do. With a steep drop off into the wooded meadows on each side of the road, there was no way she would be able to swerve around the vehicle ahead.

The more she searched for a route of escape the slower her speed became. The Suburban behind her closed its distance even more until it was nearly on top of the rear bumper, its lights splashing the car s windshield with a mind-numbing glare.

What s happening, momma? Megan cried, wiping away at the tears in her eyes.

April didn t answer. Tears just rolled down her face. She had no choice but to slow the car s speed below 40 mph, the vehicle ahead getting closer by the second.

She palmed her eyes to dry the tears, only to have more follow when the car was brought to a stop about twenty feet away from the blocking vehicle. The other Suburban veered to the right behind her, backing up and parking sideways like its twin to block the road from behind.

Four men in dark gray suits got out of the Suburban blocking the car from the front. Each wore sunglasses equipped with Starlite night vision lenses, allowing them to easily penetrate the darkness. Their angular faces were ghostly as they stood side by side in the bright glow of the car s headlights. Each was armed with a Heckler & Koch .9 millimeter SMG, a potent and easily- used weapon with a curved clip and a ball-like handle fixed on the end of the short barrel, complimented by a pistol grip that allowed its handler to spray a target with a full range of mobility.

April could feel the rhythm of her heart in her ears as the gun-wielding men stood before her. She turned to see four more men emerging from the other Suburban.

Momma, who are those men? Megan asked.

April looked at her daughter in the glow of the dashboard lights, placing her smooth hands around Megan s face. Baby, momma s gonna get us out of this.... I promise.

April looked up to face the obstacle in front of her, noting the idling purr of the car s supercharged engine, her mind pondering the unthinkable, envisioning the bodies of the four men before her flying over the hood of the car while plowing through the vehicle ahead.

A sudden rap on the passenger side window startled April and her daughter before she could enact her desperate plan. Megan screamed out for her mother, drawing away from the leathery face with deeply set lines hovering at the window.

April looked to her right in terror to see a familiar man pointing the barrel of a gun at her daughter. The nameless man that had stalked every corner of the town with his security agents on a daily basis, sliced across his neck with a single finger while pointing the weapon, gesturing for her to cut the engine immediately.

She closed her eyes, the tears coming faster than before as her head fell in a defeated stupor. She had wasted too much time thinking when she should have been acting. The engine died suddenly as she turned off the ignition, severing her hopes of escaping the nightmare she had been living in for almost two and a half years since the Omega Group s takeover of Tower Valley.

April hesitated to hit the unlock button, Megan s fearful cries reminding her of the alternate and most desperate part of her planned escape.

Another rap at her daughter s window shocked April s amber-colored eyes open again. She looked over at the window slowly, her frightened stare meeting with the man s dark and merciless eyes again.

Get out of the car, Dr. Wedding, the man demanded, his voice ringing with an accent from Europe s eastern block.

April held her finger on the door s unlock button lightly, hesitating to relinquish what little power she still had to protect her daughter.

Now, Dr. Wedding! he said, pulling back the round action bolt on the side of his HK to load the clip s first full metal jacket into the firing chamber.

April took a deep breath, wiping away the tears with her other hand. She thought her heart would burst through her chest as she hit the button, popping the locks that echoed like gun shots in her ears.

The man walked around the front of the car and stopped beside the door on the driver s side.

Momma, don t go, Megan pleaded, tugging at her arm.

It s okay, baby, she said, wiping at the tears on her daughter s face. Momma s just gonna talk to these men for a few minutes and then we ll be on our way.

No! Megan cried. Don t leave me.

The driver side door opened suddenly from the outside.

April didn t turn to look, taking her daughter s head and kissing it on top, pressing her close to her chest. I love you, sweetheart, she whispered. I love you.

Before April could finish comforting her daughter, the lead agent ducked into the car and unfastened her seat belt, grabbing her by the arm and snatching her from behind the wheel, the wails of her daughter trailing behind her.

April struggled to keep her balance while being dragged around in front of the car s headlights where four other security agents formed a semicircle around them. They looked like clones in their identical suits. Black omega symbols from the Greek alphabet were sewn on the left breast of their coats, arcing over another insignia threaded in a silver, serpentine design. Both were icons she had come to loath over the last few years.

The lead agent loomed over April, wrenching her left arm to pull her closer. Where is it, doctor! he demanded.

April grimaced with pain, but remained silent.

The lead agent looked at one of the four men closest to him, giving him a quick nod. The other agent stepped forward at the silent request, pulling out a black device similar to hand held metal detectors used in airports, complete with a digital meter and tiny sensor lights.

This was the moment April had feared, trembling as the agent waved the beeping bioscanner in front of her from head to toe, a device she had developed.

The prototype isn t on her, sir, he said, unable to find the magnetic signal he was looking for.

The lead agent grabbed April by the arm and jerked her forward again. Where is it, Dr. Wedding?

She remained silent as the tears streamed down her face, fear paralyzing her ability to speak. Months of planning their escape had been lost in her hesitation to plow through the roadblock earlier. Courage had been sharper in the preparations to flee. But such armor had been stripped away the moment she unlocked the car. The instinct to protect her daughter from being injured in a crash had crippled her choices in the heat of the moment. A moment when her daughter s very life mattered the most.

Where is it?! he shouted.

He jerked April backwards by the arm, slapping her down on the road s narrow shoulder of grass. She braced herself with the palms of her hands as she fell to the grass in a weakened stupor, blood trickling from the corner of her mouth.

The lead agent turned to his men still positioned behind the Aston Martin. Search the car!

They moved without hesitation at the order.

No, wait! the leader said suddenly, looking through the glare of the car s headlights to focus on the shadowed outline of the crying child still buckled in the passenger s seat. A Lilliputian engineer wouldn t conceal such a priceless commodity by ordinary means.

He turned to one of the darkly dressed agents to his left. Bring the girl to me!

The agent obeyed instantly, walking to the passenger side door and jerking it open. He unfastened Megan from the seat and snatched her from the car by her arm, ignoring her terrified screams.

April was hypnotized in a moment of dizzying pain, head teetering backwards onto the road s grass bank, her auburn locks spilling down the slope. She instinctively lifted a hand to the side of her face that was red from the blow as she lay sprawled on the bank, the stars slowly coming into view above the treetops through her clearing vision. Seconds seemed like hours.

A single gun shot exploded through the night air suddenly. Another sound followed, its pitch like that of something metal striking the road s surface.

April struggled to sit up on the grass bank as the marauding sounds echoed in her ears. The glare from all the vehicles headlights stunned her for a moment.

April crawled forward a bit, only to stop in a look of unbelievable horror once her eyes adjusted to the car s headlights. N.... NOOO! she screamed, looking at her daughter lying motionless in the middle of the road, blood bubbling up over the chest of her denim overalls. Megan!! Megan!!!

The lead agent stood over the child while holding a machete in his hand, HK strapped over his shoulder. He bent down and picked up the little girl s right hand he had severed with the shiny blade, tossing it into a small plastic bag. You should have never hidden the prototype there, doctor, he said, casting a cold look towards the child s horrified mother.

April cried as if panting for air.

Remember, he said. You created this calamity.

April choked on the unthinkable, face pale and death-like. The shock of the moment hit her in a wave of unpardonable guilt, eyes wide and tear-filled as she reached out towards her slain child, face puffing from all the tears.

The lead agent glanced to his left and motioned with his hand. Load up, he said, handing the blade and the small plastic bag to one of his men.

He walked over to where April was sprawled sideways on the grass on the verge of collapse while the other agents were loading up, squatting in front of her.

She bowed her head in heaving sobs, feeling nauseated by the closeness of the man s remorseless face.

You will be allotted a time of mourning, he told her in a matter of fact way. However, your presence is still required in the lab Monday morning.

He paused, grabbing her by the hair, jerking her head back to make sure she was listening. And a word of warning.... Try to run again and you will join your daughter.

He released her head with a downward push and stood to his feet. He then straightened his coat before reaching into the left breast pocket for a small business card that he tossed to the ground in front of her. Mr. Scythe is the best mortician in town, he said, his face stone-like and serious. I highly recommend him.

April cried uncontrollably as the man walked away and got into the Suburban that was blocking the Aston Martin from behind. The other vehicle passed by on the left side of the road to follow it back to town, leaving her alone with her daughter s body still highlighted in the glow of the headlights from her own car.

CHAPTER 2

Magnus walked down the long stretch of valley road at a solid pace, tugging at the lion s head cuff links fastened to the French cuffs of his white shirt. Locks of his hair caressed the sides of his bright eyes as a passing breeze bloated the split train of his navy blue coat that circled around the tops of his knees. The soles of his laced boots clicked and crackled against the asphalt that was covered in pine needles. The smallest of noises from his wardrobe were amplified in his ears, the cotton of his shirt sliding against his hardened skin, the fabric of his jeans shucking with the motion of his legs, coat slicing through the night air ushering around him in swirling breaths of distraction.

He scanned the stars while he walked, questioning in his mind why he had been led to this relatively unknown valley in Northern California. He hadn t been near this part of the state since the San Francisco earthquake of 1906; a time of judgment when the palaces of thievery and dens of whoredom of the Barbary Coast gangsters were swallowed up in the devastation. It didn t just touch one class of the city s population. Thieves, bankers, merchants, whores, commoners and the religious had found themselves all lumped together in the same fiery pit of chaos. It was a story often repeated throughout the centuries, usually involving the same cast of characters, but with little lasting effect or reflection from the surviving afflicted. Cities of commerce and residence could be rebuilt to their original splendor or even greater with hard work. But such was not the case when dealing with the depravity of mankind s Adamic nature.

A sudden rush of wind pressed against the champion while he thought about the past, gripping him with an icy embrace that stopped him dead in his tracks in the center of the road. He lowered his chin into the wind, immediately sensing an old and familiar presence. The stench of Death was scented with innocence as he lowered his gaze and focused on the road ahead of him, concentrating on dual sources of light over a quarter of a mile away. He stood like a statue staring into the night, his pupils moving with the motion of camera lenses, enlarging the appearance of a vehicle and the lone silhouette of a woman bending over something in the middle of the road.

His reason for being called to the valley at this point of the journey was at least clear, he thought. Offer hope to the stranger in the distance.

Magnus clenched his jaw and burst forward into a blinding run, literally disappearing from view.

———•••———

Magnus materialized like a ghost several feet from the crying woman, staring down at her in complete silence after having covered over a quarter of a mile of asphalt in a matter of seconds.

After all the senseless suffering and persecution he d seen visited on the weak throughout the last two millenniums, it was still almost like seeing it for the first time when he saw closeup what the woman lamented over. The body of a little girl was sprawled out in a pool of blood in the middle of the road, her right hand strangely missing.

He said a silent prayer for the grieving woman, noting the grim irony of a toy lamb clutched in the child s left arm, its curly coat soaked with innocent blood.

April cried uncontrollably, head hung in despair, the locks of her auburn hair brushing over the breast of the child s blood-splattered overalls. For the moment, she could not feel the pain of the rugged asphalt burrowing into her knees. The only thing she could feel was the stab of guilt. She had done this. She had caused this calamity just as the lead agent had told her.

His words rang cruelly through her very soul, shaking her physically. She rocked backwards on her knees, crying with desperate, inhaling breaths that struggled to pass through the swollen canals of her nose.

April glimpsed a pair of boots through the haze of tears. She fell back in a panicking fit, retreating into the glow of the headlights, rubbing her eyes profusely to see the man standing before her more clearly. His shadowy head lingered just above the line of the headlights, allowing only his tall, sleek-muscled frame to be outlined by the car s halogen beams, eyes glowing with emerald pyres.

She crawled backwards until her back hit the car s front bumper, holding her bloody hands up to protect herself from expected blows. LEAVE US ALONE!! she screamed. Just.... Just leave us alone.

Magnus said nothing. He knew words at that moment would not be convincing. Action would be the only breakthrough method. He slipped off his long coat slowly, bending over the child s body and covering her petite frame with the large garment. He then walked respectfully around the body, stopping several feet from April s position against the car s bumper.

He squatted in front of her, allowing his bronze face to be illuminated in the headlights, eyes softening in their bright glow. I will not deliver more harm to you, he said softly. I am a friend.... Permit me so to prove it.

There was a calm honesty resonating in the man s voice that allowed April to drop her blood-covered hands. Her voice trembled when she spoke. Don t.... Don t hurt me, she said weakly.

Who did this to you? he asked.

The question barely registered in April s jumbled thoughts. She looked away, wiping her face again. The magnitude of what she was involved in could hardly be explained in a fluster of tear choked words. It doesn t matter, she replied, a sense of finality teeming in her strained voice. Nothing matters any more.... Meg.... Megan is gone. I broke my promise.... I couldn t save her.

Magnus glanced back at the covered child, pausing for a moment of silence at the mention of her name. A coldness welled up deep from within, visiting him with a familiar sorrow.

He looked back at April, quickly wishing away the image of his murdered wife before it clouded his thoughts. He cocked his head to the right a bit, training his augmented hearing on dual sounds in the distance. The low hum of two powerful V-8 engines whispered in his ears like a passing wind.

With a gentle and hasty movement, Magnus grabbed the grieving woman by her shoulders. I won t hurt you, he reassured her, looking into her wide eyes as she gasped with an expression of shock from the sudden gesture, appearing as though she had just noticed him. I m going to put you into the car until I get back.

Who are you?

The cavalry.

There s nothing you can do, she replied, her head falling to the side again. The Omega Group is too powerful....

Magnus expression hardened even more with her words. The Omega Group? What are they doing here? he asked in surprise.

She did not answer.

Magnus lifted her off the road with a look of urgency, experiencing no resistance as he carried her to the passenger side door of the car. He opened it and placed her in the seat where her daughter had been sitting earlier, reaching across her to flip off the headlight switch to snuff out the sight of the child s body still lying in the road.

Magnus grabbed the keys from the ignition and knelt beside her. Stay in the car and keep the doors locked, he said, pushing the universal lock button in a hurried breath. I ll be right back.

April said nothing. She simply looked out the driver s side window, defeated.

Magnus closed the door and put the keys in his pocket.

He walked to the rear of the car and eyed the long road before him with a hardened stare, fixing his hearing on the sounds of the retreating vehicles again. His body stretched forward in a hazy blur as he broke into another lightning run, disappearing from sight.

———

The yellow lines on the long stretch of road blurred together in one wide bar beneath Magnus hypersonic feet. His arms and legs were distorted and wavy in his race across the asphalt, the wind shear rolling over his bronze face, hair whipped straight back. The trees on each side of the road merged into seventy-foot-tall picket fences in the wake of his speed, the stars above him running together in streaks like wet paint on the night s dark canvas.

Several miles ahead of him, traveling single file at steady rates of 60 and 70 mph, were two Suburbans, their red tail lights glowing like afterburners.

Magnus honed his focus on the rear vehicle and closed the distance easily, cutting his velocity in half to keep from overshooting the target.

The tinted windows on the vehicle s rear double doors shattered as Magnus plowed into the right side tail light with his left shoulder, shearing away the quarter panel like wrapping paper. The Suburban swerved to the left on impact, tires squealing as it flipped over into a violent roll down the road s left side bank, headlights twirling in every direction. The SUV crashed upside down into a cluster of pines, killing all four men inside instantly.

Magnus didn t watch the Suburban crash behind him, moving quickly to overtake the other vehicle ahead before the occupants inside had a chance to respond to their comrades sudden demise. He leaped forward in an arc over the Suburban s rear doors, tucking his knees into his chest while sailing over the long roof in cannonball fashion. He kicked his legs straight down once he cleared the windshield, the oval toes of his boots piercing the vehicle s hood like a pool of black water, sheet metal rippling all around him as he hammered through the engine, ripping gashes in his boots and the sides of his jeans as he pushed the V-8 block halfway through the pavement.

The vehicle jolted to a deafening stop, as if slamming into a brick wall, its rear end flying up off the ground. The lead agent burst through the windshield head first from the passenger s side, flying by Magnus in a shower of glass, hitting the asphalt face first in a fifty-foot slide. The other agents were killed instantly as their heads slammed against the roof of the bouncing vehicle.

———•••———

A hushed silence of death shrouded the valley road around Magnus as he stood unmoved at the center of the hood s crater, boots resting on top of the V-8 engine that was driven into the pavement, legs wet with antifreeze and transmission fluid. He was gazing into the open portal where the windshield used to be, its crumpled edges surrounded by a border of jagged, glass teeth. The twisted and bloodied bodies of the other three men were sprawled across the tops of the seats.

Magnus turned toward the road where the lead agent lay groaning with muffled, dying breaths. He punched through the rippled sheet metal in front of his waist with his fingers, gripping the hood from underneath, tearing it down the middle in a single shear that echoed throughout the surrounding forest. He took a step forward and kicked through what was left of the radiator, booting the entire front end, bumper and all, several hundred feet down the road.

Magnus walked slowly over to where the man lay dying, his boots grinding glass and other small debris into the road s surface with his forceful steps.

He stood over the man briefly, his emerald eyes bright and merciless, fists clenched at his sides.

Magnus tucked his left boot under the man s right arm and flipped him over, barely recognizing the leathery face that was ground to a bloody pulp. Phinehas Kaiser, he said in a low voice.

Kaiser, a ruthless network operative and lead agent of the Omega Group s Sentinel Corps, lay helpless at Magnus feet, spinal cord severed, right eye torn from its socket. His left eye was half-closed, the scope of his vision blurred and dense, confusion overwhelming him as fiery tentacles pulled at the very essence of his hardened spirit.

Magnus bent to one knee, drawing close to Kaiser. He grabbed him by his blood-covered throat.

Kaiser choked on his own blood as the mysterious enemy lifted his head and shoulders off the pavement. The vision in his remaining eye cleared enough for him to see Magnus bronze face. He didn t recognize him. But he did recognize an other-worldly mystique in the stranger s phantom eyes only a select few of his superiors in the group had displayed in the many dark rituals he had participated in during his employment.

That s right, said Magnus. You don t know me. But I know you, Phinehas Kaiser. I have watched your kind from behind the scenes for nearly two thousand years. Brazen and merciless puppet masters of nations. Cowards who manipulate the weak while dancing on strings of your own, controlled by powers more wicked than yourselves.

Magnus grabbed Kaiser s chin with his other hand while holding his shoulders off the pavement. Why did you kill that woman s daughter?

Kaiser kept a disciplined silence with what little strength he had.

Why is the Omega Group here in this valley? he pressed.

Kaiser tried to force a refusing smile between the stone-like fingers that gripped the sides of his chin, clinging to his silence as if to insure his place in the next world.

Magnus would not push the issue any farther. Keep your allegiance to your dark masters, then, the champion replied. But know this, Kaiser. I am of the Ancient World.... I share in a legacy that was once a plague upon the mighty Philistines. A legacy that sheds the blood of evil men both great and small.... Men who have no reward in eternity.

Magnus spun Kaiser s head around with a quick twist of his hand just as a look of terror welled up in the agent s remaining eye, the bones in his neck snapping loudly as his face was turned toward his back.

The champion stood back up and let Kaiser s turned face crash squarely into the asphalt.

He lingered in the middle of the road as blood dripped from his fingers, watching a small portion of the road beneath Kaiser s head liquify, turning counterclockwise. A plume of black smoke billowed from the opening as the sides of the small hole hardened for a moment, the smell of brimstone filling the air. The back of Kaiser s head collapsed slightly with a quick suction emanating from the gateway, pulling his soul-crowned spirit down toward Hades.

Magnus turned and started back down the road while the portal closed behind him in the same liquid motion as it had opened. He could hear the distant cries of Kaiser s spirit descending into torment, mixing with the echoes of blood dripping from his fingers that splattered against the lid of the agent s asphalt casket.

COMING SOON...

Book One entitled:

WAYFARER
THE SHEKINAH CHRONICLES

ISBN:0-7684-2234-5

The forces of darkness have been struck a devastating blow at the hands of the risen and ascended Christos Champion. Yet Lucifer, the fallen Morning Star, is not about to give up. With the tide of war turned against him, the Dragon Lord goes on the offensive, striking out at humanity with his most fiendish and dangerous designs. At the command of the Most High, the archangel Michael brings forth the last warrior of the Shekinah Legacy. Born to an incredible destiny and raised from birth to be a warrior, Magnus the Lehohn is transformed from a mere human into a living weapon—a sword that will pierce the heart of darkness itself. Infused with strength, speed, and supernatural sight, this betrayed and exiled Roman warrior will come face-to-face with the greatest threats humanity has ever known.

From the Roman battlefields of old to the richly detailed landscapes of the present, Magnus must use every one of his unique abilities and finely-honed battle skills to weave his way through a complex tapestry of devious plots, deadly traps, and bloody battlefields. But before he can face the demons without, this Jewish Prince must quell the turmoil within-or risk unleashing a terror against which no man or angel can stand.

Book Two entitled:

ASCENSION
THE SHEKINAH CHRONICLES
ISBN:0-7684-2243-4

Prepare yourself for a ride that will take you from one end of the galaxy to another in a riveting battle for the Kingdom of God.

Book Three

THE SHEKINAH CHRONICLES
ISBN:0-7684-2244-2

Witness the Day of the Lord as the Christos Champion returns like a thief in the night.

Book Four

THE SHEKINAH CHRONICLES
ISBN:0-7684-2245-0

The rise of the Millennial Kingdom is sure. But an old hatred is stirring under the guise of submissive subterfuge.

Book Five

THE SHEKINAH CHRONICLES
ISBN:0-7684-2246-9

A secret society has arisen at the halfway point of the Millennial Kingdom. The Covenant Harness has been rediscovered. The past is taught, but little is remembered.

Book Six

THE SHEKINAH CHRONICLES
ISBN:0-7684-2247-7

The tides of war are mounting. Arm yourself for the
final conflict, for the Abyss has been opened.

Book Seven

THE SHEKINAH CHRONICLES
ISBN:0-7684-2248-5

Bear witness to the Great Judgment as you are taken on
a journey through time and eternity.

DESTINY JUNCTION
ISBN 0-7684-2062-8

Destiny Junction is a small town, not unlike any other small town in America. As its name implies, however, it becomes the place where many people's lives meet destiny.

Through one young lady's obedient Christian life and the work of the Holy Spirit subsequent to her murder, the lives of many people in the town of *Destiny Junction* are transformed.

This is their story…a story about life…and what it means…or what it ought to mean.

SHADOWS OF LEGION
ISBN 0-7684-2201-9

Their dark legacy dates from before the dawn of recorded human history. Their reach echoes through the ages, an evil too terrible to comprehend and a strength to rival the greatest angels of heaven and the foulest of the fallen in hell. They are Legion, a horde of countless demons acting as one, united in mind and purpose.

When Scott Macklin's father dies, Scott begins to uncover the secrets behind his father's involvement with a mysterious group known as The Shadowed Ones. With a conspiracy of dark forces pressing in from every side, Scott finds that he is not alone in opposing Legion. He is joined by Douglas Prichard, a dedicated military commander; Father William Los Cruzado, a priest with a shady past; and Dr. Rachel Walters, a skilled hostage negotiator.

Together they must face this force of darkness known as Legion. With little but their faith to guide them, they must hold back a rising tide of evil that threatens to consume the souls of all mankind, without falling prey to their own human failings.

ANCIENT LIGHTS
ISBN 0-7684-2167-5

In the aftermath of a devastating earthquake in the Middle East, a young Bedouin makes a remarkable discovery. After stumbling into a long-buried cave, the young boy uncovers a sealed urn-the contents of which could change the fate of the world.

Conspiracies and intrigue abound as the discovery of the Urim and Thummim—the ancient lights of Israel— are thrust into the spotlight of the world stage. Lost for more than 2,500 years, the twelve multi-colored gems quickly become the center of the ongoing battle between good and evil. Nations are pitted against each other and a corporation will risk everything in a desperate struggle to control the supernatural power of the *Ancient Lights*.

Available at your local Christian bookstore.

SAVING GRACE
ISBN 0-7684-2204-3

As the only daughter of a successful businesswoman, Grace grew up with nothing but the best. Sheltered by her single mother and educated in an exclusive private school in Detroit, Grace was not ready for the harsh realities of an unforgiving world.

Grace's naivete coupled with her desire to experience life on her own terms leads her down a path of emotional devastation and physical abuse. Through a chance encounter Grace meets Mike, a successful design artist who introduces her to a relationship very different from her usual one-night-stands and affairs with married men.

Things take a turn for the worse however when Grace's roommate walks in on her and her married personal trainer in their apartment. This betrayal tears apart Mike and Grace's romance and shatters the trust and friendship between Grace and Trina.

In the midst of torn relationships and a life-shattering loss, Grace is left with no one to turn to except the God she thought had long since abandoned her.

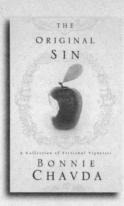

THE ORIGINAL SIN

ISBN 0-7684-2181-0

The *Original Sin* is a series of fictional vignettes illustrating how the spirit of jealousy, the original sin, works in the lives of humankind. The three short stories will put into historical perspective the comprehensive and cunning results of the venomous bite of jealousy's fangs.

You will be drawn into the fictional drama of these biblical stories as you watch the deceptive pull of jealousy in the lives of Cain and Abel, Sarah and Hagar, and Judas. Their stories will be a warning to all to avoid the vengeful force of the 'green-eyed monster.'

Available at your local Christian bookstore.

UNDEFEATED IN LOVE AND WAR
ISBN 0-7684-2221-3

Jack Denova is the most feared and respected no holds barred fighter in the world. His record is 402 wins and no losses in the dark underworld of no rules, no rounds, and no judges, mixed martial arts, cage-fighting. He travels the world for hire, displaying his talents to anyone for the right price. He is 38 and at the top of his game when a run in with the Russian mob and accidental killing of one of their top men puts him in the custody of the FBI.

After a failed attempt on his life while in prison, the Russians kill his parents in a brutal act of revenge. Jack's world in shattered and he decides to turn states evidence and testify against the Russian mob family, leaving him in protective custody of the FBI.

As Jack waits to testify he plans an elaborate scheme to get revenge on his parents killers, turn the tables on the FBI, and start a new life with a woman he has grown to love, who is also being hunted by the Russian mob.

Throughout it all, Jack must deal with the brutal consequences of his former life, while using the warrior inside of him to fight for a chance at a new one.

CHRONICLES OF THE HOST
Exile of Lucifer
ISBN 0-7684-2099-7

Lucifer, the Anointed Cherub, whose ministry in heaven is devoted to the worship of the Most High God, has become pessimistic about his prospects in heaven. Ambition inflamed, he looks to the soon-to-be-created Earth as a place where he can see his destiny realized. With a willing crew of equally ambitious angels, Lucifer creates a fifth-column of malcontents under the very throne of God. Hot on their heels, however, is a group of loyalists, led by Michael and Gabriel, who are suspicious of Lucifer's true motives. In detective style fashion they slowly start to unmask the true nature of Lucifer's sordid plot.

Chronicles of the Host is a fantastic novel of the beginning of all things. Follow Lucifer's deceptive plans to rule over Earth and his inevitable fall from grace.

MASTER POTTER
ISBN 0-7684-2172-1

This exciting two book allegory, *Master Potter* and *Master
Potter and the Mountain* of
Fire, addresses the current fas-
cination with supernatural
phenomena. The secular mar-
ket is flooded with power
encounters, New Age, occult-
ism, angels, demons, witchcraft
and sorcery. There is a
renewed hunger to move in
supernatural power, reflected
in the wildly successful Harry
Potter series.

Master Potter tells the
story of *Beloved-wounded* and left vulnerable by an
abused childhood, she is rescued by Master Potter.
Whisked away to his rustic home overlooking the quaint
village of Comfort Cove, Beloved begins her painful journey of healing.

The hardships she endures, the lessons she learns,
and the invisible world she discovers will cause you to
cheer for each triumphant step she takes and weep with
each mistake she makes.

Master Potter is a powerful Christian allegory for
all ages with the potential to become a Christian classic
along the lines of Hannah Hurnard's *Hinds' Feet on High
Places* and John Bunyan's *Pilgrim's Progress*.

GLAD TO BE LEFT BEHIND
ISBN 0-7684-2961-7

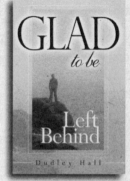

A group of teenagers are tragically drawn together after the suicide death of one of their classmates. In their deep searching for answers to his death they are all drawn to Uncle Herm. Uncle Herm was their friend and mentor. Herm was easy to search with and they met with Uncle Herm on a regular basis.

They were a no-name group until one day Paul came rushing in to the discussion with a frenzied look. He had been listening to some radio program proclaiming that events in the Middle East were ripe for the battle of Armageddon to begin right away. This sets the stage for the rest of the book as these group of kids and Uncle Herm explore all of the 'hot topics' of the endtimes: Israel, Antichrist, rapture and of course the big one, Armageddon.